To dearest Victor...

with much love,

Liberation at Long Last

"Seek and ye shall find"

Mary

M. Mallia

Copyright © 2014 by M. Mallia.

ISBN:	Softcover	978-1-4931-4168-5
	Ebook	978-1-4931-4169-2

All rights reserved. No part of this book may be reproduced or transmitted in any form or by any means, electronic or mechanical, including photocopying, recording, or by any information storage and retrieval system, without permission in writing from the copyright owner.

This is a work of fiction. Names, characters, places and incidents either are the product of the author's imagination or are used fictitiously, and any resemblance to any actual persons, living or dead, events, or locales is entirely coincidental.

This book was printed in the United States of America.

Rev. date: 03/29/2014

To order additional copies of this book, contact:
Xlibris LLC
0-800-056-3182
www.xlibrispublishing.co.uk
Orders@xlibrispublishing.co.uk
521389

Liberation at Long Last

Chapter 1

It was a crash-landing! Who would have thought that parking his car in the city centre car park, he would come back to find it written off—a total loss. He wasn't speeding or suddenly stopping in traffic or dodging the potholes in the roads—for heaven's sake his car was allegedly parked safely in the city centre car park! Nor would he get any compensation as this would be deemed as an 'act of God'. An act of God for what? An act of God to punish him? To punish him for what? Like everyone else on this Earth, he had his faults, of course, to which he admitted and never tried to shy away from, but deep down, he was one of the good guys who tried to do good and avoid doing bad when and as often as possible.

He had set off that morning whistling to himself and thinking how sweet life had been since this new girl had entered his life. She appeared as if from nowhere, and he didn't know much about her, but she had touched something deep within. Although he had only known her for a few months, it felt like he had known her all his life. A friend, lover, companion and soul mate, maybe? He was now oblivious to the offhand comments his colleagues made at work to undermine his authority. Oblivious to the noise outside his house at weekends as the house next door was being demolished and rebuilt. Oblivious to the heat and the smell of sweat everywhere and on everyone. He was well and truly in love and nothing else mattered!

He had walked with a song in his heart and a sense of gratitude that surpassed the mundane. This morning was totally unexpected, like a bolt out of the blue! A bolt, indeed! Where had she fallen from, this demented, mad woman? It's true that people who decided one fine day to end it all had to do it somewhere, but to crash-land, bum bang right onto his car and crash right through his roof was a bit more than he could comprehend that morning. He would have to see to believe.

Who was this woman, anyway? Of course, the phone call at work from the police made everybody want to make fun of him, and teasing comments of misconduct, possibly of a sexual nature, were rampant! He had rushed to the scene but hadn't been the first one to get there. The police were there already, the ambulance was there (how futile for someone who was so obviously dead!), and lots and lots of people! Relatives, maybe? Curious passers-by were ushered to move on by the police. Exclamations of horror, lamentations, and crying resembling that of an angry, frightened animal that had just been maimed filled the air. Suddenly, it seemed much hotter, and the stench of sweat seemed more prominent than ever before. The stuffiness of the air, the heat, the sweat, the noise all suddenly began to get hold of him, giving him a feeling of being slowly smothered and making it hard for him to breathe.

It wasn't a pleasant sight to behold, let's face it! The car was indeed a total loss. The bodywork crushed. You wouldn't have realised that one human body crashing at that speed could cause such damage—but hey, there was the evidence staring him in the face—fact, not fiction.

The colour red! Not his favourite colour, of course. He always preferred blue. When asked, he always undoubtedly went for blue, without hesitation. But today, red seemed to be the colour of the day and splattered over what had just been his beloved metallic blue car, was red everywhere. It was hard to comprehend that all that red could come from just one dead body. He was sure that in Hollywood movies in which everything is over the top, the amount of blood shown in casualties was quite realistic.

Why was he thinking of colours? Of movies? Who was this woman anyhow, who on this day had decided to end her life and ruin his day in every way?! Couldn't she have fallen on one of the cars on either side of his, maybe? Why his? He did feel as if life had been singling him out on this occasion and was hoping that this spate of bad luck didn't come in threes! Could he afford a new car? With Christmas just five days away and most of his Christmas shopping having been left undone, life wasn't seeming so sweet after all, and the whistling and singing in his heart seemed to be suddenly fading away, as was the colour from his face. He fainted.

Eventually, as he came round, he hoped that it had all been a bad dream and that suddenly his girl would come and soothe him. Her kind words and melodious voice and her warm smile and twinkling eyes would be enough to bring the blood rushing back to his face. Alas, when he opened his eyes, the same scene he had been so keen to blank out faced him once again with a vengeance and was as large as life!

It was only then that he began to wonder who this woman could have been. Surely, she was someone's daughter, wife, mother, sister, friend, helper, and acquaintance. She must have fulfilled some sort of role in life which had made her important, if not indispensable to some people! For a moment there, he stopped his thoughts in their track as the shock of that thought caught hold of him. He suddenly realised that it could have been his own mother, his own sister, his own wife, his own lover, his own friend, his own lovely, kind-hearted, dark, beautiful girl! It seemed as if for a moment he forgot about his car being a total loss and about not having money and a car for Christmas and was touched—for a moment—by a deep compassion.

He looked carefully at all the people who had been gathering there now. The young fair lad, with hazel green eyes, leaning carefully over the shattered body caught his eye. This young fair lad let out an anguished whisper of 'Mum, why?' and burst out crying. It started off like a soft sob but became louder and louder, and gradually, his tormented cry filled the stuffy, stench-filled air. It was heart-breaking to watch a young lad who was barely eighteen lose his mother like this and finding her like that! His heart went out for him, although he did not know him from Adam, and this tragic accident had cost him his car, his Christmas shopping, and a lot of money and had upset his peace and quiet.

There was something about this lad that continued to captivate him. He wished he could read what was going on in his heart and mind just by looking at his hypnotic green hazel eyes. Of course, he couldn't, but he could only imagine. Ah, compassion! He had been trying to be compassionate and put himself in other peoples' shoes all his life and had managed on occasions to do this well. He wasn't so sure about today, though, as who can actually put themselves in that lad's shoes today?

Possibly, like him, this lad had set off for his day's work with a song in his heart and a spring in his step. Possibly, like him, this lad had up until that moment in time been happy with his life and the little blessings life had been throwing his way. Possibly, like him, this lad had been looking forward to a good, productive working day with some fun to follow in the evening with family and friends.

Possibly, unlike him, this lad would never recover. He would be able to get a new car, somehow. He would manage to get the Christmas presents sorted, somehow. And he would regain his peace and tranquillity as soon as he went home to his sweetheart. But, the life of this nameless lad with the deep green hazel eyes had been shattered forever. And just as that motionless, shattered body would never regain life, that boy would not regain the innocence, the joy of living that had been now shattered, any time soon.

The first question that we all ask is, 'why'? Why this woman? Why this lad? Why today? Why my car? Why a few days before Christmas? Couldn't she have waited a few more days when his car wouldn't have even been in the car park as he would have had time off work? Couldn't she have done it later when he would have clocked off? Or earlier, when he wouldn't even have arrived? All these thoughts, amongst many others, raced through his simple mind, filling it with a cluttering noise which began to hurt.

Yet again, he thought how selfish to have these thoughts when he would soon walk out of here and barring money for a new car, his life would be back on track in the next couple of weeks. Yet, the life of this lad leaning over his mother's dead body might take many years to get back on track. This lad left the house in the morning hoping it would be a morning like any other and yet, it was the morning where the rest of his life would change forever! A moment in time, one single act committed in one single moment changing the course of many lives forever. He hoped and prayed that he himself would not have to ever face such a tragedy as he wouldn't be able to show half of the courage, half of the love, half of the emotion that this green-hazel-eyed lad had shown. He saw in this lad's eyes, heard in his cry, smelt in his breath the love he had had for this woman—his mum who had ushered him into this world. He perceived immeasurable anguish and torment, yet the love that this lad had had for this dead woman lying in front of him was undeniably visible, shining through the pain. He decided that no son should ever have to see the woman who had loved him all his life and whom he had loved since forever in such a state.

He continued to wonder if there had been any other family members present, possibly others that hadn't heard, yet and hadn't seen. He felt for them although he didn't know them. His heart went out to family members who hadn't yet been told. Who, maybe like the rest of them were at work and it was business as usual when they were suddenly hit by this bombshell. He felt for these people for whom a moment in a day can shatter and change their lives as they know it, forever.

Will his curiosity ever be satiated? And why did he have this urge to know, anyway? It wasn't as if it was any of his business really, was it? His race was always being accused of being busy bodies, minding everyone else's business, but never attending to their own and making other people's business their own. Maybe, he wasn't as liberated as he thought he was! But, compassion was there manifold—a good sign for a person trying to open his heart and bare his soul to the human condition of misery and pain.

Chapter 2

Her spirit, one the other hand, hadn't left the scene. They always say, and many people believe and this might be true—that especially when one dies an accidental death (was this accidental?)—their spirit hovers for some moments or days even until it moves on to another realm. She had wanted to run; she had wanted to hide, but her spirit wouldn't go anywhere. It hovered over the aftermath of her actions.

She watched astounded by the fact that she had finally found the courage to do what she had wanted to do for the last ten to twelve years—to die! They say that you need more courage to live than to die, but they didn't know what they were talking about! The courage to die was true courage. The courage to die, to face an unknown reality an unknown state of being and leaving behind loved ones was a courage that only came through, through what exactly? Was it courage? Was it despair? What was it? Anyway, it was too late to sift through all of that now, as her body shattered the peace of the car and all of those left behind. She could remember, however, calling out the name of her eldest daughter as both her feet left solid ground. Why had she done that? It's not as if her eldest daughter could reach out and save her now? She knew that her eldest daughter had been trying to save her for most of her living life. She knew too, that if it weren't for her and for her most beloved green-hazel-eyed youngest son, she would have done this much sooner. She knew that forty-three was no age to die! And yet, it was no age to live as unhappily as she had. For a split second on her way down, she had felt liberated—totally and utterly liberated! Until her body crushed through the stationary car, that is.

She suddenly realised, as her spirit hovered over the scene, what a catastrophe she had caused. It dawned on her now that it was too late and that she couldn't turn the clock back, that maybe this was a mistake! That maybe there had been a way out of all that suffering and pain a way that did not involve taking her own life. Had she tried hard enough? Explored every alternative? Looked at it from every different possible angle?

She made her way to where her youngest son was as he leant over her mutilated, lifeless body. She tried to dry his tears. She whispered softly in his ears telling him how much she had loved him all those years, telling him how much joy, love, laughter and fun he had brought into her life. He kept her company when she had been lonely, and she loved it when they went out together and people would think that he was her boyfriend. Why can't he hear her now? Will he ever know in his heart of hearts that none of this was his fault? Will he ever know that all the love that he had lavished on her would never be lost? Would he ever be told how much her heart leapt with joy when his keys turned into the front door as he let himself in ravishing, asking for food? Would he ever know the pleasure she felt in making him the most deliciously filling meals even when she was listless, tired, and depressed? Would he ever be told that he was the bright light shining in her darkness, a song that her heart sang, a treasure which she valued beyond words could ever describe, and acts of love ever measure? Would he know that on numerous days he would be the sole reason she would drag herself out of her hypnotically calling bed? How will he ever find out now that he was the love of her love and the life of her life? Who will tell him?

She had never wanted to burden him with her troubles and her sad life story. It was a lot to bear for her, for her eldest daughter too. But him, she had wanted to spare him at all costs. She hadn't ever let on to him how depressed she had been, how her life had been failure after failure and disappointment after disappointment, shattered dreams and shattered promises. She had wanted to love him as she had never been loved. She had wanted to nurture and keep him safe as she had never been herself. She had wanted to protect him from her sadness and pain from herself and her heart-breaking reality.

Giving birth to him had been a doddle compared to when she had done it seven years earlier to her eldest daughter. In the latter, she had thought that she was going to die and that her body would give in and completely collapse leaving her lifeless. She hadn't been ready to die then, not at barely eighteen years of age. Now, at twenty-five, surrounded by family and friends, she was ready—to give birth, not to die. Giving birth to him had been a ray of hope in this mundane and harsh reality she had created for herself, and now looking back in hindsight, he was the best thing that had ever happened to her. As he grew older, he continued to be a source of joy and a ray of hope which made her heart flutter with joy and gratitude at having been given such a gift of which she had felt utterly and truly unworthy.

The birth of her eldest daughter was another matter. She had been barely eighteen at the time and totally unprepared for motherhood. For who is at that age? She had hoped she would be able to go to college and to study to become a school teacher. Becoming a school teacher in her country and in that day and age had been quite fashionable and she had the grades. She had always passed her exams with flying colours and all her teachers had urged her on. However, her dad and her destiny had other plans for her, and she would live to regret not having stood up to her dad and taking the easy way out in the future. She hadn't planned on getting married so young and having a daughter at barely eighteen. But it was a fait accompli and that was that!

She hadn't spared her eldest at all! Why? Why such a compulsion to protect the youngest and expose the eldest? Where was the fairness in all that? She could see it now as her spirit could perceive her eldest daughter at a stranger's house throwing up in their toilet at the breaking of this devastating news, lying on the floor in a heap overwhelmed and overcome by guilt, desolation, and utter despair. Hadn't she loved her eldest daughter in the same way she had adored her youngest son? She would need to suspend judgement on that one until the time was right.

This actually was now getting a bit too much for her to bear. She decided that the reasonable thing to do at this point in time would be to wait. To wait until her judgement was due and hope for the best! It was no use trying to sort out, judge, and analyse her intentions and her actions now; it was pointless at this point in time! She would have to hope that the God she believed in would judge her less harshly than she was judging herself just then and that He wouldn't take too long in coming either.

Perhaps, the God she believed in was a merciful God after all and would forgive her what she wouldn't and hadn't forgiven herself. Perhaps, this God was much more compassionate than she could ever comprehend! Perhaps, rather than throwing her in a place where she would be eternally damned, this God whom she believed in would eventually welcome her into His kingdom when the time were right. She had yearned to enter His kingdom all her life. After her two-year love affair with Greg she had hoped He would forgive her, and her loving God in whom she had vehemently believed did. He had sent her signs and signs and more signs telling her loud and clear that she had been forgiven. Her sins were forgiven. Her two-year love affair with her husband's best friend waved away as if by a magic wand or rather washed away by bloodshed by One whom she believed had died for all. So, why couldn't she then forgive herself? Why did she have to torment herself and beat herself up every day with futile feelings of guilt? Why hadn't she seen then how useless feelings of guilt and self-condemnation were? Why hadn't she been able to love herself as she had loved her two beautiful children? Why hadn't she trusted His forgiveness? All these questions, and more, crossed her mind as her spirit continued to hover over the havoc her simple action of her feet simply not touching the walls of the walled city had caused.

She might have to wait for judgement for a while, although she hoped against hope it wouldn't be a long wait. She always envisaged that judgement took place instantaneously, but of course, this was just her fancy and wishful thinking. She might be judged on the other hand and then have to wait until she was completely justified and purified before she could enter His kingdom. She wasn't sure what the procedure was and who would guide her to where she needed to go and who would support her now. The only strong feeling she got was that she had to wait and that there would be a lot of waiting in store for her.

Things weren't moving fast here, and she wasn't going anywhere in a hurry. She had always had the patience to wait. She had been a very patient person in life. She would wait for her husband to leave the house in the morning before she got up. She would wait for her children to go to school so that she could go back to bed. She would wait for enough money to buy new furniture, a new car. She would wait for friends to come round to keep her company and spare her her own. She would wait for someone to wake her up inside . . . she would wait for passion and perhaps love to return . . . but, they never did. Finally, hope gave way to despair, and she would wait for death!

To wait . . . and to wait . . . and to wait . . . and why the thing that she had waited for and wanted most in her life never came, she could never understand. There was no doubt she was patient, but life was taking the mickey at this point, and she was going to show it who was boss. She would wait no longer. She would not wake up in the morning hoping she wouldn't anymore. No, sir! Those days are over, and the waiting has finally been stopped. She hadn't bargained for having to wait in this state of nowhereness, nothingness, not knowing how long she would have to wait for either. Aha, life was in control after all. There seemed to be no escape of this waiting neither here nor there.

Oh dear, there he was! She hadn't really bargained on how she would feel when she saw him, big, dark, and with the stench of sweat and fear intermingling. She didn't want to actually see how much he had loved her. She saw and knew but tried not to perceive in her heart of hearts how much pain and anguish she had caused this simple, humble fisherman. He had loved her. She had been the best thing that had ever happened to him in his life. When she was around, he came alive. His heart felt things he never thought his tough and rough exterior would allow him to feel. And yes, she had touched his heart and opened it to love. His eyes told of his love and devotion as his mouth constantly uttered her praises.

It's true she had had an affair with his best friend for two years, but he was willing to let that go and start again if only she would let that happen, if only she would love him again. Would she ever be able to love him again? This is a question he asked and she asked herself time and time again. What would it take for someone to fall in love with the same person all over again? This was part of the torment of her life. Maybe, deep down inside, he knew too. But, it was something he kept hidden and didn't want to see. It was much easier believing that she would love him again, and that indeed, she did. It was less heart-breaking to believe that his efforts to keep her were bearing fruit.

She, on the other hand, thought it was much less painful to pretend. By pretending that she could love him again, he would be less hurt and would feel that his efforts were not futile and that the love of his life was loving him back, finally! Finally, she was his and he was hers. But, would they live happily ever after?

She never gambled that as soon as her feet left solid ground and her being was lifeless, shapeless, and formless she would see it all as clear as daylight. What she thought she had known before what she had wanted and needed to know. She had allowed herself to see what would cause her and him the least pain, but what she saw now was the truth, the painful awful truth that she had never loved him, could never love him and would never love him and that he didn't have a clue. Respected him, yes as he was an honest, honourable, loyal, hard-working husband, and she had a lot of respect for him. But, love? Love was a matter of the heart and not the head, and she always knew she had not been true to her heart for many, many, many years for as long as she had cared to remember, really!

She knew it but couldn't see it because to see would cause more pain than this pain she had just endured as her body had crashed through the metal of the car. 'The truth will set you free,' someone had once said. Did they mean now on Earth, or thereafter? She wondered if there were people out there who lived life truthfully—authentic people were they called if she remembered well? People who had been true to their hearts, bearing the pain as it is not hiding from it or creating a greater pain to run away from the real pain in their hearts. Well, she had to conclude that authenticity hadn't been one of her strengths in that case.

'What would happen next?' she wondered. The pain of knowing this truth in her soul of souls (her heart was shattered by now and had bled to death) and seeing it in the depth of her very being was unbearable. Moreover, a perception about the pain that this had caused and was causing also began to take hold of her spirit little by little until she didn't know what to do, where to go, and who to turn to.

Luckily, her guardian angel, whom she had prayed to daily during her life on Earth, came to her rescue, offering her comfort and reassurance. He held her hand so that she would not be afraid and tried to reassure her with his loving presence—no judgment came from him. And how would she be judged and by whom, she still did not know. She wondered and pondered, and it came to her suddenly that it will not be in the way she thought she would not by an old Man, with a white long beard, wearing a long white robe sitting on a white cloud . . . .

No, she would create her own judgement and be in a state of waiting until all of the pain she was feeling now and all the suffering she had caused would abide, subside, and be allowed to go. Her guardian angel told her that she was not allowed to enter into His Kingdom until her own pain, her daughter's pain, her son's pain, her husband's pain, her mum's pain, her dad's pain, her brother's pain, her friends' pain, her neighbour's pain . . . all the pain and suffering was dissolved and allowed to go. 'And until then, you just have to wait, Amy!' she whispered to herself.

Chapter 3

In the meantime, she could only watch, wait, and see! She had never thought that this simple process of watching, waiting, and seeing would be so unbearable. She had thought in her other life—the one in which she had inhabited a human body—that this is precisely what she had been doing. And to a certain degree she had. She saw and didn't like what she saw and shielded herself from it. However, it created more pain to shield herself from the original pain and so on and so forth until the resulting pain shielding her from the original pain had become so unbearable and insurmountable that she had to call it a day!

So, why was it still so utterly painful? Where had all the defence mechanisms she had used so well in her lifetime disappeared to? Is this what this waiting does to you? You are left defenceless, and you are made to see what you don't want to see, to hear what you have been shutting your ears from for many human years, and to know what you knew but didn't trust and denied! To come to the original pain, the original source of the original pain to the core of her being was what she had been trying to escape—yet, here there was nowhere to run to and no stories to fabricate and no more pain to shield from the original pain.

It was getting boring and long drawn. It began to dawn on her that time was now measured differently on this side or 'the other side'. She had no way of actually telling how long she had been in this waiting place or state, shall we say. It was tricky. It already seemed like an eternity, but she was sure it couldn't have been that long. How would she be able to tell? Who would help her now? She would have to cheat and find a way. She had got used to getting her own way on the other side—the label of being 'mentally ill' had served its purpose well, then—but, not now!

As her human body was being transported from the scene of her death to a hospital mortuary nearby, she peeped at the watch on the paramedic's arm, and it showed it to be 1 p.m. So all of this waiting was only one hour's worth?! So is this what eternity is where time goes on forever or never? This wasn't what it was cracked up to be. This didn't match her idea of the afterlife as a state of utter and total bliss where her soul would be liberated, her heart soothed, and her pain dissolved forever, in an instant. That is what she had hoped to achieve by allowing her body to be smashed to smithereens—save her soul. She hadn't bargained for this waiting and watching and seeing.

Now she was being given the chance to see things as they really were, she wasn't sure she wanted to be able to see. How blessed are the blind. How blessed to have eyes and not be able to see. How damned to have sight and have to be able to see. To have eyes and be able to see is imbibed by a sense of responsibility . . . Oh, not responsibility! She'll have to wait a long time if she is going to be made to look at that. Oh no! Her eldest daughter had believed and at times accused her of getting away with murder under the guise of having been labelled as mentally ill. Had she been right? Had she used that label to get away with it? To get away with being totally selfish, self-absorbed—shunning the needs of others always in favour of her own. Concerned only with her own comfort, rest, and well-being? Responsibility was a heavy theme she would have to come back to. She said to herself, 'Another time!' And time seemed to be the only thing her soul possessed at the moment, so much of it that it verged on infinity.

'So what happens when you own the faculty of eyesight but choose not to see? What happens to your heart, mind, body, and soul? What happens to the people around you—the people you confess to love and the people who lavish love, affection, time, and attention on you? What happens to the people (possibly like her eldest daughter) who had given her life—a life for a life!' she thought.

The ambulance came to a sudden halt with a jolt. She had never noticed the potholes in the road as much as she had today. Maybe, her husband had failed her in so many ways but in one way had been a very good driver and either avoided the potholes altogether or drove so slowly and carefully that he eased the bump every single time.

She watched in awe as her desiccated body was transported into the cold, morbid mortuary. Well, it wasn't exactly the Hilton Hotel, was it? What was she expecting, a seven-star hotel as you get in Dubai? A part of her had hoped that it would have flowers on the walls, that it wouldn't be so cold in there, and that she would see familiar faces to soothe and comfort her.

And the familiar faces did come. They didn't look happy, comforting, or soothing. In fact, she wasn't quite sure whether it was anger or fear she depicted at that point in time in their sad faces and heavy hearts. She wasn't sure if her eldest daughter would be there. She had called her name as she descended with great speed—that cry—was it regret? Was it that just as both feet found themselves kicking in mid-air she had had a change of heart? No, it had felt like total and utter freedom for a split second. But, freedom *always* has to come at a price, always! And what would the price be this time? She pondered.

So many questions and so little answers—yet, she had an infinity, it seems to sort them out. So her idea that life after death would be sweet tasting like manna from heaven, a country overflowing with milk and honey was a fallacy? She couldn't even get it right this time round. Will she ever win?

Hang on, what's he doing here? She was grateful for the distraction, she had to admit. No more watching and having to see. She can't take her own judgment anymore—it was too cold, too harsh, and too direct. Her own judgement of herself didn't beat about the bush. It pointed a finger, a finger at her! Yet, when her body had been strong, healthy, alive, and well, her finger had always pointed in the opposite direction. It had pointed in the direction of her father, her mother, the lover who spurned her, her husband who loved her, life, circumstances, fate, destiny—it had always been 'out there' never 'in here' and always 'them' and never 'me'.

Anyway, what was he doing here? He was a part of why she had done this and maybe he knew it. He was one of the reasons why she had had to do this, and yet if the wedding had gone through, all of this would have had been in vain. How futile! Who did he think he was, looking at her as if he knew her, as if he got her, as if he cared? All he had cared about had been getting her eldest daughter to marry him. Well, this should take care of that, as after this unexpected turn of events, she wouldn't want to marry him and she would have saved her eldest daughter (unbeknown to her eldest daughter, of course!) a lifetime of misery and pain.

She seriously doubted if this young lad with a heart of lead who had never shown any emotion had been capable of love. Her eldest daughter would need a man with passion burning in his heart, body, and soul—a man who would fall head over heels in love with her and who would love her unconditionally, protect her, and take care of her every need. She knew her eldest daughter much more than her eldest daughter ever knew herself. She knew her needs more than her eldest daughter knew her own needs. She knew her eldest daughter, and her eldest daughter knew her. That's why they couldn't get along. They showed up in each other every single trait in themselves that they were trying to hide from themselves and from everybody else. They highlighted each other's weakness and vulnerability so much that it was scary for one of them to look at the other as they might see things that they didn't like which they knew were also there in themselves. It was actually like holding up a mirror and what you looked at is what stared back at you—there was no escape.

A doctor—he wants to become a doctor?! Her daughter would marry a doctor who would take care of other people and their needs, heal and cure other people, and be pleasant to other people but would not do that for her. She knew it, but how could she tell her eldest daughter? Her eldest daughter hadn't believed her whenever she had tried to hint at the subject and had always thought that she had had an ulterior motive. And she had had, maybe! Yet, now her daughter would open her eyes and see, and if this didn't stop the wedding from going ahead, then nothing will.

The man she had called 'husband' for many years was there too. He had loved her, and she could see it as clear as daylight in that sordid, dark, cold room. She saw it so clearly that her heart ached with the pain he was feeling. How was it that she had never perceived that before? Was it at all possible that his fits of rage, anger, and fury were all down to a fear, a fear of losing her, a fear of actually never having had her. Maybe, just maybe in his heart of hearts knowing she had never loved him. Maybe, just maybe he knew but chose to protect himself from that knowing.

It's amazing that when someone pretends for such a long time, for so many years, they can't begin to tell the lies from the truth. Living a lie becomes so habitual that everybody begins to believe that lie and that lie becomes their life. The lie takes on a reality, becomes solid in shape, and determines people's every decision and their every move. It protects temporarily, but eventually ends up causing much more pain as the person's heart and mind are so far removed from what is real and from what is true. And if the truth will set you free, what does living a lie do, then?

Is this what had happened to her? Is this what had made her actually mentally ill? Was this what being mentally ill actually is? The great disparity between what she had perceived as reality and wanted to embrace as reality and the reality itself. She hadn't wanted to live that reality, no way. She went on with her everyday business going through the motions of daily life on autopilot and out a sense of duty, she guessed. Her body was there performing the tasks of cleaning, cooking, ironing, baking, cleaning, cooking, ironing, baking, shopping . . . Yet, her heart and her mind were back in her home country, Down Under. Her heart and her mind had been stuck for the last twenty years in a time warp where she had been embraced by her lover Greg shutting out the rest of world, daring and not caring.

She had never recovered from that, and whatever reality she was faced with, she wasn't there, she wasn't present—she was in Greg's arms yearning for his passionate kisses, sweet and tender caresses, and silent whispers of proclamations of undying love. She could still feel his slender, soft, pink fingers running a shiver down her spine as they slithered up and down the erotic parts of her naked body. She could still feel his lips softly, yet passionately kissing the nape of her neck, coming down to her chest, down to her small, yet firm breasts (she hadn't breastfed, so they hadn't sagged), making her go wild with lust and passion. He had liked running his dexterous fingers through her short, dark hair amongst other sensitive places on her body which made her writhe with excitement and filled her with utter and sheer ecstasy. It all always seemed as if it had just happened a moment earlier, not twenty years prior to that. She swore she could still smell the fragrance of his perfume as it had lingered on her naked body. Her whole body sometimes had felt as if it had just been touched by his kisses and caresses and just the thought set her on fire. These thoughts never left her, day or night. They were as real as real can be, much more real than the food she would be eating, the hot chocolate she would be drinking, and the chocolate cake she would be baking. More real than the broom she would hold whilst sweeping the house, more real than the bread she would freshly bake every day and its smell as it wafted through the house filling it with a sweet smelling aroma. More real than her daughter, son, or husband.

It was what filled her reality in the day and her dream state in the night. Like an obsession, it would not let her go. Or rather, being obsessed, she would not let it go. It seemed like she couldn't, but maybe it was that she wouldn't. Some would argue that she couldn't let it go. Others would disagree and say that she wouldn't let it go. Either way, she was bound endlessly in this raging sea of thought and emotion being tossed and turned in a dark, deep sea of yearning for what was, could be, or could have been. There had been no rest for her mind and no respite for her soul. The electric shock convulsion treatments (which had already been made illegal in most European countries at this time), which had been administered many times to make her forget, seemed to make the distant past much more present and real and the memories much more vivid and the need to go back much more pressing. That is where she had wanted to be. She had never wanted to leave. He had promised he would leave his wife, but like many men, he was a coward and not keeping his word was what had destroyed her. He had shattered her dreams, her life, and her hope for love, security, passion, and protection. Protection? Protection from what or whom exactly? Even if he could protect her from her angered and humiliated husband and his fury, he would never be able to protect her from herself and from the hell on Earth she would eventually create for herself and for all of those around her.

It hadn't mattered that they had been both married at the time, that they both had children, and that Greg and her husband had been best friends. None of it mattered! They both had everything to lose, and what would they gain? The love, the lust, the passion, the stolen moments in which they were lost in each other's gaze. Their lives could be shattered in one moment in time, just one moment is all it took, and they would be found out. Yet, they didn't care that they could be found out. They didn't care for as far as they were concerned it was all worth it. They were young, reckless, and in love and had the audacity to believe that true love would conquer all evil and melt away all the pain. That's what she couldn't take in her embodied life! How come love did not conquer all? How could he leave her, abandon her, and act as if none of this had mattered when it came to the crunch? He chose his wife over her—the wife he had so bitterly complained about time and time again, the wife he would slag, the wife he would proclaim to not love over and over again. Yet, had it been love true love, or now come to think of it, was it merely lust, passion, a bit of fun on the side?

All this thinking, wondering, and asking had made her very tired. She longed to shut her eyes and go to sleep as she had done for all those years. Shutting her eyes and sleeping had been the story of her life. She chose when to wake up, if to wake up at all, when to sleep, how long to sleep for, when to open her eyes, and how long for. Well, actually, it wasn't her who had decided, was it really? Thanks to the advances in medicine, chemicals pumped into her body to numb her mind were doing it for her! Blessed, blessed, and more blessed are the peacemakers who sleep and slumber. She thought that now she would be allowed to sleep forever. Not for one minute had it occurred to her that this was the point of no return where she would have to stay awake with eyes wide open to see and ears unplugged to hear and maybe even listen if she waited long enough.

Her reverie was thankfully interrupted by someone who seemed to get paid for covering up lifeless bodies—what a way to make money! Coming around checking up on them one by one on tiptoes. She couldn't fathom why someone would tiptoe in a room full of corpses; it wasn't as if they were going to be woken up, was it? Or rather, it wasn't as if they were ever going to be allowed to go back to sleep—ever again, is it?!

Chapter 4

This was too much for her—how is she going to survive being awake the whole time? And this wasn't like watching tellies, either. Watching tellies always managed to numb the pain, the most excellent way to see any other reality than your own. Bliss! The modern opium of the people, perhaps. To be stuck in other peoples' messes and pain always seemed to put yours in perspective, somehow. People like to watch others struggle. They seem to get a kick out of the suffering of others. It seemed to make theirs seem insignificant. But, here it was different. This was watching what you really did not want to see and you were given no choice about it. You just had to stay there with your eyes wide open, ears unplugged, and watch whether you liked it or not.

There were no TV guides to offer choice upon choice upon choice, identifying when the same programme was going to be repeated if you missed it the first time and switching channels if you got bored out of your wits. Not that people seemed to get bored nowadays. People seemed to be getting dumber and dumber and less and less discerning as to what makes good TV viewing in her humble opinion. The more 'real', obscene, rude, and loud the people on screen are, the more successful the programme became. A shame really. Anyhow, all in the name of free will and freedom of expression, I suppose. Yet, how free were they really?

How free was she really? Hadn't she thought prior to being here that she would be free forever? Free from all this thinking, analysing, judging, naming of intentions, actions, being pulled in different directions by conflicting emotions, and free from guilt, from the mundane, from things that didn't matter, or shouldn't have mattered, but did. Free from attachments to the past that bound her by this invisible anchor deeply embedded at the bottom of a deep, dark sea from which there seemed to be no escape. Free from the longing of being back in her lost lover's arms, free from the longing of being kissed and caressed by him, free from the memories that seemed so present and real taking over her present life and dictating her every thought. Free from the soul-destroying routine of everyday life where one day seemed so similar to the other, with nothing new, exciting, or mentally stimulating happening. Free from her own self-judgement which was not sympathetic to her story—'a saint with a history' she would call herself on one level—'in your dreams' her harsh self-judging voice would mock! Free from her desire to sleep and slumber day and night, shutting herself from herself, from her self-judging voice which never seemed to cease, tire, or retire. Free from her desire for peace, tranquillity, and calm, which it seemed the more she desired the more they eluded her. Hadn't that Man she had believed had died to save all of Mankind promised 'Peace on Earth to all Men of goodwill?' It's true she wasn't a man, but wasn't that just a figure of speech meaning that the peace he was offering was for everybody? Why had she been missed out? Why was it that the harder she tried the more she failed? Didn't goodwill mean that she did not wish anybody any harm? Of many things she had been guilty during her life on Earth, she never, ever had wished anybody any harm, not even her harshest critics and worse enemies.

It was a heart-breaking sight which stopped her in her musings and jolted her back to the present. It nearly broke her heart to see all those people gathered together in one place to commemorate her life and give her soul a good send-off.

She wasn't sure about that. What does a good send-off actually mean? Who were they doing it for? Was it actually for her that they were gathered there, or for themselves—a way to connect to their own pain through someone else's? In actual fact, did it really matter to her why they were there?

They had turned up for some reason or another—end of story. It wasn't her job at this point in time to judge them; it would be her job over the next many moments of forced, continued wakefulness to judge herself, however. Would she judge herself the way she had when her body and soul had been one? Would her self-judging voice still be as strong, as opinionated, as obstinate, as unforgiving?

Anyhow, it felt as if anybody and everybody was there—the whole island, it seemed. Family and more family, friends and more friends, acquaintances and more acquaintances, people she had liked, people she had utterly disliked, people she had been totally and utterly disinterested in, people who had brought her pleasure, people who had brought her pain, people who had valued her, people who had devalued and humiliated her. People, people, and more people. She didn't even know that so many people knew her.

Anyway, from where she was standing—well, not actually standing—she couldn't explain at the time what position her disembodied being had assumed—this was all a bit too much for her to bear. As if she suddenly saw (not realised of course, at this early stage), just caught a glimpse of the enormity of what she had done, the impact not just on close loved ones of course, but it seemed she had shaken the very village and a big part of the island to the core. She would have to pay for this in some way, but how, she would have to wait to find out.

She was beginning to have an idea of what shape and form this atonement might take the waiting seemed to be one way, the seeing what she didn't want to see, and the state of constant wakefulness another way. She had a gut feeling well, now that she didn't have a body anymore, she wasn't sure if she could call it a gut feeling that this state of being wasn't going to last forever, but she wasn't going to a better state of being anywhere soon, not until all this sh** (not that she should swear in church) had been cleared and her soul would be cleaned, cleansed, and made as white as snow.

She had hoped that by 'crossing over to the other side' as so many people referred to it, her life as she knew it would come to an end. She hadn't bargained that it would have to get worse, much worse before it actually got any better. Having waited for so long to die, she would now have to wait goodness knows how long to live.

Oh my goodness! There he was again, a dark, well-built man with a tough exterior as his manual jobs demanded, yet within whom a soft, tender, and compassionate heart had resided. He had been so handsome in his youth—a 'teddy boy' in those days with a long curl casually drooping over his tanned forehead. His deep, dark eyes had always been his best feature though. It was as if all the overflowing love which his heart couldn't hold came shining right through his eyes. He was a good man. She knew that. But, she had been so wrapped up in her own little world and in her own losses and pain that she had never really given him and how he felt much thought. She actually blamed him for all her misfortune most of the time. Why such a pang of pity now? What good was that going to achieve? She tried to move as close to him as she could to see what she could catch a glimpse of in those dark, mysterious eyes a sadness, pain, anger, fear, guilt maybe? No. No. No. It was much worse. Much, much worse and much more painful to see, *love*. She had suddenly realised he had never stopped loving her, never.

As he sat in the front pew waiting for the funeral service to commence, he remembered the first time he had laid eyes on her. She had been the most beautiful girl he had ever seen, and he had seen many since he was a very handsome, charming, and honest young man. He had girls falling at his feet back in his home country blonde girls, dark girls, young girls, older girls, well off girls from well to do families, less wealthy ones but he had never been interested. His mum had given up on him. To every girl's mum who had approached her, hoping that her daughter would be the lucky one, she would say to give up hope as he wasn't interested in dating or getting married. He was too busy fishing and getting himself into trouble playing pranks on unsuspecting passers-by and innocent local fishing boat owners.

When even younger, his mum was the one who wore the trousers in his family home, with the money and the business acumen, whilst his dad a very quiet and shy, yet good man would go about his business silently. Whilst she hustled and bustled running the village grocery shop, he welded ships at the local dockyard. There were many things that united them, but one thing that did divide them and cause them endless sleepless nights arguing and that was their eldest son Mike. They both agreed that he should be sent to a public school as they were not academic themselves but very well off and wanted him to have the best start in life. On this at least they did agree and they did put up a united front. Uniforms were tailored, school satchels ordered, school shoes bought from the capital—ready for the big day.

But how would he be made to go? He was as stubborn as a mule and hard-headed and believed that school was for wimps and for people with nothing better to do in life. Life in the great outdoors, underneath the eternal clear blue sky, constantly whiffing the fresh salty sea air is what he believed in—the school of life in the long run taught him all he needed to know and all that an academic school would have never have been able to.

He flatly refused to go to school and played truant so many times that you could say that school wasn't going to be the way forward for him and the money his mum and dad were spending would be totally wasted. When he did go, of course he was so rude to the teachers and got so severely caned that he wouldn't be able to walk for a week and would go fishing instead.

Fishing had always been his passion. In fact, his mum thought he would never get married as he was in love with the sea—the sea had been the love of his life. He bought, made up, and sold numerous boats and was well known in that neck of the woods for his dealing and wheeling in boats. He was known to have 'borrowed' or rather stolen a boat or two on occasion for a night or a few and avidly remembered for burning one just for fun.

There he would forget the world and all its cares, all the pressures to conform, to perform, and to succeed. He didn't care for any of these. All he had ever wanted was a quiet life in which he could fish and be happy. Whether he would ever fall in love or not, he did not know but one thing he knew was that he had to be by the sea. When he was out at sea, he felt such peace; you could almost say he felt like a spiritual awakening every time he was out there as if, his whole being came alive in a sea of calm, tranquillity, and peace. He made it seem to an untrained layperson's eye deceptively easy, as if a night at sea were a doddle. He never grumbled how hungry he was when he returned to land at four, five, six o'clock in the morning. He never complained how his shoulders, back, and neck ached after lifting tons of swordfish and tuna into his modestly sized boat. He would be too elated, filled with such a sense of achievement, of pride, not pride as in arrogance, but pride as in the satisfaction of a job well done, in working honestly for a living, making his own way in life depending on nobody but himself and what life decided to provide him with that particular night.

He often wondered when out miles away from any sign of human habitation how his life would unfold. One thing that he was quite clear about was that he had wanted to be independent. As much as his mum and dad had loved him, they were old school and very strict, controlling, and smothering at times. Conform, conform, conform had been his dad's motto. Well, he would do anything but that! Wasn't conforming the same as dying while you were still living? What was the point of life if you didn't explore the endless possibilities, push your own boundaries, and dare to be different? 'I am not a sheep,' he would say to the sea in the dead of night as the stars watched over him and the sea provided for him.

It came as a shock, however, to his dad more so than to his mum when he had announced that he had bought a one-way ticket to the land Down Under. Many people had left the island in search of better prospects down there, and they knew of many friends and relatives who had upped and left their homeland in search of a better life. For him, it wasn't so much a better life as much as being a rebel, independent and wanting to make it completely on his own. He was a free spirit and his dad's nagging to conform had scared him out of his wits. He had looked at his father at times and vowed he would kill himself if he ended up like him. He was hard-working of course and a very respectable member of the local community, regular church goer and a dedicated family man. He, on the other hand, was a bit more like his mum, who wasn't going to be your regular stay-at-home mum like many of her contemporaries. No, she would run a business, the local food store, which was actually part of her home, and make a lot of money for the family. As if that weren't enough, she would be sewing half of the brand new dresses worn by numerous females on the first Sunday of August during the well-esteemed and much anticipated village festa.

Her heart wasn't in the village festa this year, however. Her eldest son was leaving. She didn't know when she would ever see him again. She had loved him like none other of her children, which is not really fair as a woman should love all of her offspring equally, surely? But, no matter how much she rationalised in her head, her heart pounced with joy every time he called her 'Ma'. He would leave the week before the village festa which means that this would be the first village festa she would have to bear without him. It's true he had always been getting himself into mischief and had neighbours threatening to kill him as he had burnt their cat alive, burnt their boat, or burnt their dog a bit of an arsonist, really when you come to think of it. He would take refuge and sleep in the mortuary nearby many a night, to escape his father's fury, knowing that his dad would beat him black and blue as soon as he heard of his yet new prank. When asleep in his bed, he would take a bite to eat and rest his weary head by the foot of a cold metal bed on which a cold dead body lay. There had been times when it was too cold, so he would ask his unsuspecting brother to sleep in his place—swapping sides, he would silently chuckle inside. This was a clever and clearly premeditated move to make sure his brother would get the beating in his place. By the time his dad would realise, his brother would already have got quite a few of the lashings intended for him. This would buy him time to pounce out of bed and dash out of the house like a man possessed. And sometimes 'possessed' seemed to be quite an accurate description of him, many people in the village would agree. But, he was her son nonetheless and she couldn't bear to imagine her life without him.

She had bought him the best suitcase on the market and showed a very brave face in public. She smiled as she proudly announced to her regular customers that her eldest son was turning a new leaf; some sense has been knocked into him and he was going to emigrate to find work. However, that smile was only to hide the pain of her impending loss. What was there to be proud of really? He would go and only God knew when she would ever see him again. Her husband, on the other hand, would not talk about it, not with her, not with his own brothers and sisters, not with his friends, (not that as a busy family man he had any friends really), not with his colleagues—not with anybody. He just went into himself as if this was the death of his eldest son and he needed to grieve. Perhaps, a part of him felt responsible for this loss, as he had been a disciplinarian as most dads were in his day and age and his free-spirited son would not have any of it.

The big day arrived and was gone in a flash. He'd enjoy the voyage which was going to take about four weeks on that massive ship that had pulled up in the harbour a couple of days prior to the big event. There were tears of sadness, loss, words wishing him luck, words giving him advice, and words hoping the best for him from all and sundry.

Needless to say, he was a youth just turned eighteen full of a zest for life, adventure, and new beginnings. He felt courage in his loins and hope in his heart. His gut ached, not from fear but from wanting to go and conquer the world and be who he was meant to be—fulfilling his destiny. His gut ached, from the yearning to be himself and do away with all that pressure to conform from a small island where everybody knew him, he longed to be on this continental island where he would be a nobody. He stood up long and tall on the front deck counting his blessings and longing for the new life that awaited him ahead. He did not know a word of English, did not have a job lined up in advance, there would be nobody to meet and greet him on the other side, yet he had a vision which emboldened his steps and gave courage to his heart.

If only he had known then what he knew now! How his dreams would one cold sunny, winter's day be crushed to pieces and all the events that would lead up to that one moment which he could never have foreseen—he probably wouldn't have ever set foot on that godforsaken continent of an island. If only he knew then, that the quiet, simple life his soul had always yearned for was far more likely to materialise on that small island in the middle of the Mediterranean Sea rather than there, Down Under. How he would give his heart to one woman, to be crushed and trampled upon. How she would use and abuse him. Yet, how he would never stop loving her.

And now bearing her body as it lay motionless in the coffin, it all seemed to him as if he were watching a film in black and white of someone else's funeral. Not his beloved Amy's funeral, no. A stranger's funeral. This couldn't be happening to him. She would not do this to him and to them. She would always be there. As the coffin arrived at the altar and was put down on the cold marble floor, he couldn't help but wonder how it had all come to this!

Chapter 5

He had always got himself into mischief his whole life, but he longed for the love of this woman. He knew she would be the making of him and because of her he would be a new and better man—reformed even. Don't get me wrong, he was naughty but not nasty, not a nasty bone in his body. And as to his heart well, it was unusually open for a man his age open to love and to be loved to be transformed by the power of love into an even happier, more fulfilled being. He longed to make her his own. He was on a mission to win her over and to make her his forever.

So there she had been minding her own business at the bus stop, and he would suddenly start chatting her up. She was shy, coy, and very young and very beautiful. How old could she be, sixteen, maybe? He was twenty-one, but at the sight of her every time, his heart pounded with love within him and a yearning deep inside to get to know her, be with her, and maybe one day marry her even. This was what filled his day and night dreams. He would imagine his life in pictures, in colour not black and white. How happy she would make him, and how happy he would make her. Young love, his first love and in his eyes, she was perfect. In his eyes, their life together would be perfect. Other people's marriages failed, maybe. But, they would live happily ever after.

He wasn't academic and could hardly read and write but was picking up the English language quickly. He was a fast learner. He was determined. Luckily for him, he was able to befriend one of her brothers so that in the end he set him up with her. He didn't think his life could be this happy, this perfect. He knew now what his heart had been destined for and what all the great films depicted when it came to love the passion within, the perfection were all his for the keeping as she agreed to marry him after only a short engagement. He couldn't believe his luck. He was the happiest person on earth and would say this to anyone who cared to listen. She was going to be his, and he was going to be hers. As far as he was concerned, there had never been any other and there would undoubtedly not be any other until he dies. Whilst this notion would fill most people with dread, it only filled him with a sense of awe, of how lucky he was to have such a beautiful being to give himself to and who had chosen to give herself to him.

The moment he held her hand at the altar and had her proclaimed as his wife, he felt the proudest and happiest man on Earth. It was a simple wedding. She wasn't into a lot of fuss this woman. She was the embodiment of perfection in his eyes and could do no wrong. His love for her was unfathomable, and he was always sure of her love for him. This was forever. He would be hers for keeps. There was no turning back, but that was OK because he didn't at any point until now want to turn back anyway. If this was as good as it gets, then he was fulfilled and would be forever.

That word forever is a hard one as many of us know. It was only after four years of marriage that she declared that she had been having an affair with his best friend Greg. It had been going on for two years right under his very own nose, right in his face, and right under his very own roof! He wasn't even sure he believed her actually. A Brazilian author once wrote that people don't believe you when you have the audacity to speak the truth—they would rather believe a lie or something like that anyway. And it's true. He decided he wouldn't actually endorse that truth unless he saw with his very own eyes, heard with his very own ears, and experienced with his very own being the affair she had claimed had been going on. He had been convinced it was all a story to get him jealous and start giving her a bit more attention and TLC as that had lapsed over the last couple of years.

He would keep watch, he had decided, like they did in the films he had watched at the drive-in with her. He would spy on them—as unless he caught them red-handed in the act, he would not believe. And so he did.

And so they did. That fateful day, that obscene scene would haunt him every day for the rest of his life. As hard as he tried, he could not etch it out of his living memory. He wished there was something that would erase it, wipe it out completely and make it vanish into thin air as if it had never ever happened, but instead of getting fainter, the snapshot of what faced him that day grew stronger and took hold of him. Those carefree days were over. A fury controlled his every action now. The days of innocent freedom were gone.

He changed inside. On the outside, it was business as usual, but on the inside, he felt numb, dead. On some level, it seemed that a devil had taken hold of his soul and would torture him forever. His whole inner life was shattered his heart utterly and completely broken. He was out of his mind with the questions that had faced him that day. That she didn't love him anymore seemed obvious. Had she ever loved him? Had she loved him on their wedding day? Why did she marry him in the first place? Did she seek Greg out? Did he seek her out? Did it matter? Did he still love her? Would he ever be able to get past this? Would his heart ever heal? Would he ever be able to forget about this? Would he ever be able to forgive her? He was a man tormented being pulled in this and that direction by the desire to forgive her and the urge for revenge and punishment. It felt as if he were going mad. The fury he felt was in direct proportion to how much he had loved her, doted on her, and trusted her. He was no mathematician, however, he knew that that hadn't been reciprocated in the same way.

The only solution he could think of would be to go back home to his home country which he had never missed and had hoped not to return to in a hurry, not in circumstances such as these, anyway. But he had to leave; he had to go. And, he wasn't going anywhere without his little one, his little Marie! They had a four-year-old beautiful daughter by then who had been the apple of his eye. The sleepless nights drove him mad, but she was the apple of his eye, nonetheless, and he didn't think that he could love another human being with such an intensity as he did this tiny creature. She, on the other hand, his Amy well, not his anymore, would not let him go and take her with him without a battle. She wanted to stay, to stay and keep her little

Marie with her. He wanted to go, to go and take his little Marie with him. It was a battle of wills, fought over by a desire to make the pain go away for neither of them wherever they turned to could find any respite or peace day or night.

Having Marie hadn't been easy. It was a difficult pregnancy, and she thought she would die during childbirth. Having been born at only seven months, she had been in a hot cot at the local hospital for the first eight weeks of her life until she recovered and was able to be taken home. It was hard work without a shadow of a doubt, but Amy had had her mum's support and her three brother's dedication to her, and to her little Marie had been invaluable. One brother would buy her toys, the other lovely clothes, the other would take her out, and the other would feed her playfully when she didn't want to eat. In that respect, Marie was surrounded by such love for the first four and a half years of her life, which was very lucky as there were hard times ahead for her and she needed all the love she could get!

The house was sold quickly and cheaply. The tickets booked. The ship boarded as they headed to his home country. The four-week voyage was hard. He still loved her, which he couldn't deny. The love he felt for her at the altar, he still felt now. Although the heart that contained that love had been shattered, it had been as if the love itself had multiplied. He had been ready to forgive her and move on. So why hadn't he? What was stopping him? That picture! That picture in his head as they both lay there naked lost in each other's embrace moaning and groaning with pleasure, passion and lust! His beloved in the arms of another. If it had been any other man, maybe he could have got over it quicker, but his best mate! Some mate! His wife and his best friend! And this wasn't even a film he was watching for entertainment's sake this was his wife, his life.

He had thought that being back home would ease the pain and make the memory go fainter, disappear eventually and lose the hold it had on him. How wrong could he have been! There was not one day, that that scene would not cross his conscious mind. And not once, mind you, but many times a day. What to do? How do you escape from yourself, from a demon that seems to be taking hold of you, possessing you, owning and tormenting your very soul? Work. He had worked it out. Work. Work. And more work. He kept himself so busy that he wouldn't have any time to think and to look at his own thoughts. And when not working, drinking. Ah, the benevolence of being drunk. What balm to his mind and spirit. No image, mental or otherwise, would get passed the drink. No. This was the way forward. Sadly, he discovered that the senses were numbed, the mind blanked but the raging demonic fury, anger, and hatred inside could not be tamed no matter what. They would burn inside his body like molten lava under the Earth's crust and like a volcano every so often, very often, would erupt when Marie was still only little. These eruptions happened regularly. It seemed like the activity of this volcano grew stronger and stronger and the eruptions became commoner and deadlier. There were casualties, of course. The sofa would be shattered. The fridge murdered. The plate smashed to smithereens. The food splattered on the ceiling and the floor. And the heart and mind of little Marie murdered, filled with terror and dread for her own safety and for the safety of her beloved mother and little brother.

The other casualty, of course, was Amy. How could such intense love coexist with such extreme anger, fury, and hatred? And how can one person coexist in peace with such constantly, conflicting emotions? He couldn't bear to think of those times when he had completely lost the plot. The scenes in which he would hurt her physically and make her cry, humiliate her, judge her were now playing in his head as he looked in the direction of the wooden brown box across the aisle. They were making a jarring, loud, squeaking sound which got louder and louder and which would make him scream, hadn't he been sitting in the very front row of a stuffed church in which people were as squashed as sardines watching his every move.

The organ began to play. The opening hymn. What had his Marie chosen for this? He was very proud of her much more now than he had ever been. She was going to read the First Reading at her own mum's funeral and thanking people for coming at the end—that takes courage and fortitude. He knew that his beloved daughter, who had made him so proud, possessed both. It wasn't until she was older and stood up to him and showed him that she wasn't taking his mad outbursts anymore that he had started to respect her. On that day, she had met mettle with mettle, and she was only fourteen. He never had thought she could be so brave, but she had shown admirable strength and for that he had to respect her. It's as if stooping to his level, shouting at him and stamping her feet she had finally reached him in the recesses of his own self-centred existence, where he nursed his pain and where nothing and nobody had been allowed. Yet, on that day, she had found a way in. She had to stoop to his level, of course, but she found a way in, nonetheless. From then on their relationship blossomed as he recognised this was no ordinary daughter for if she had the guts to stand up to him, him who she was petrified of she could stand up to anyone in life.

He nearly killed her once. And suddenly as she stood up there reading the First Reading, he was overcome by an immense sense of shame. This daughter had brought him nothing but happiness and joy. She had loved him beyond words could say. And yet, over two mouthfuls of lemonade which she had drunk when he was out fishing, he had nearly killed her. After a night's fishing, finding out that some of the lemonade had gone missing, he blamed his youngest son. But no, it wasn't him, Amy had convinced him. 'No, it couldn't have been him, Mike. It had to be Marie. It was definitely her.' So he marched to her room breathing heavily, a rage bubbling up inside growing stronger as he got closer to her. She lay in her bed terrorised and frozen in fear as his heavy, angry hand reached over her innocent body which was beaten black and blue. At five o'clock in the morning, sweating from a night's fishing, the demons tormenting his soul took hold of him, and once again, like a man demented, he was striking. Why had he done that really? Who was it that he had actually wanted to hurt that day? Did she still remember? Had she ever forgiven him? Had he forgiven himself? He looked up and there she was reading at her own mum's funeral. He wasn't sure how well he actually knew her at this stage. But, he was proud of her, nonetheless. She had held it all together and given him a strength. They had suffered together, and he knew she loved him beyond belief. The sense of shame grew stronger and stronger until by the end of the reading he began to cry silently, tears forming and filling the whole of the eye, on the cusp on the verge of falling onto his dark, weathered face.

She had been the backbone of the family. She had shown admirable fortitude. Not only had she got a degree from the local university, the whole village, yes the whole village literally adored her. All the mums had wanted their sons to marry her. She was a very altruistic person and had been doing voluntary work in a local children's centre since the age of fourteen. She had read in church and during important festivals in church and outside the church where hundreds of people would gather since the age of eleven. Wherever he went, he would meet someone who would be singing her praises, and this, of course, made him a very proud father. None of this was any of his doing; of course, it wasn't because of him, but it was in spite of him. And he knew it. And that knowledge hurt. He could attribute some merit to himself regarding her education, but regarding her popularity, her standing in the community that had all been her own doing with the help of some friends, of course. But not from him. To give him his due, however, he would attend any ceremonies and initiations she would be taking part in to show his support. He looked at her with a mixture of admiration and pride. He looked at himself with a growing sense of shame.

He also had a son. Well, they had had a son together Amy and himself. Born seven years after his little Marie. Born on the island now. Born out of the desire to forgive, to make it work, to maybe win her love back as she had been adamant that she had wanted another child. For Marie, she would say, 'For Marie.' It's not right that she should be on her own all her life without a sibling. Life could get very lonely, and Marie would have nobody to turn to. Besides, Marie was whining day in and day out about how she longed for a sibling. He himself was hesitant, but he would do anything to please Marie and win back the love of his Amy, so he surrendered. And there he was the cutest, fairest, most delicate beautiful baby anyone could lay their eyes on. They would call him Matthew as he was a gift of God and would continue to be to her a gift of God for the rest of her life. Matthew grew in stature and grace and had a really good relationship with his mother but didn't quite get along with his father and his father didn't quite get along with him. It was a shame really, but there was a gulf between the two that could not be narrowed no matter how hard either of them tried. It was like when one tried, the other turned away; when the latter would try, then the former would turn away and never shall the twain meet! Well, never say never, for as long as there is life, there is hope, they say.

He didn't know whether he felt a bit envious of how much love Amy lavished on this boy who seemed to be the centre of her universe, the beating of her heart, and the spirit of her soul. Maybe that was it. In her eyes, this boy could do no wrong. In her eyes, he, Mike, was wrong the whole time. The more he tried to win back her love, the more she drew away. When he stopped trying to avoid the pain of rejection and disappointment, she would accuse him of not caring, of not loving her, and of not giving her the affection and attention that she needed. She hadn't been an easy woman to please, that's for sure. He was damned if he did and damned if he didn't! Whatever he did was wrong in her eyes. Yet, this boy this hazel-eyed most handsome boy could do no wrong in her eyes, and for this, he was aware of a growing sense of envy, bordering on jealously. Maybe, he even felt that this boy was a threat, putting a wedge between them being the cause of this seemingly growing rift.

This didn't stop him from supporting the boy in his career and helping out when needed. But the boy hadn't wanted his monetary help. He had yearned for his approval, for his unconditional love which now he couldn't give not to his son, not to his daughter, not to his wife, not to anyone! That might be something he might not be able to give ever again. He loved his son more than words could tell, so what was it that had stopped him from showing it in a way that the boy would understand? He himself had been a boy too, once, and he knew what he had wanted from his own father—not his money, not his reprimands and beltings, but his approval. Unfortunately, that was the one thing he never got. It left a void in his life, a sense of there being something missing in his heart. Why was he doing the same to his son? Why couldn't he love his son in the same way he had wanted to be loved by his own father? He knew what he had to do, but these demands seemed too much as he was constantly grappling with his own pain and couldn't accommodate their pain, their needs, and their unspoken demands. He needed so much and had nothing left to give.

It was the pain inside, the constant nagging in his heart as to whether she loved him or not which had accompanied every heartbeat day and night. Was she just using him to stay in the house with the children? Was he kidding himself thinking that she would ever love him again, if she ever did in the first place? The torment was too much to bear and the answers didn't even bear thinking about, but this continued to add to the bubbling, the building up, and the eruptions of his inner volcano. No matter how calm and quiet he seemed on the outside, the slightest incident like an unexpected noise from one of the children or a little less lemonade in the bottle would set him off into a frenzied rage where he would lose control of all his rational faculties and lash out, physically hitting whoever was there, physically assaulting any furniture or any appliance visible, and verbally cursing so badly that it seemed like Satan himself were present in the house. When he was at home, everybody felt frozen, afraid to talk or move for fear of setting him off.

And now, it's like a completely different man sitting in the front row of the church. Being exposed to his own pain, his own vulnerability had been something he had vowed to himself he would never do, ever again. He had to protect himself with a leaden suit of armour. Otherwise people would just crush you, trample all over you, and after they took everything you've got, leave you bare, naked with nothing left for yourself or for anyone else—he used to say to himself! He truly believed this. He believed that after having given her his heart, his love, she had taken it, crushed it to pieces, and left him with nothing. Yet, before he had had so much to give. Now sitting in the front pew, he broke down and cried. He's not exactly sure what he's crying for. For what could have been, maybe? Self-pity, perhaps? A sense of futility?

He hadn't cried in years. In fact, the last time he had cried had been many years before when he had been watching a documentary about poor people and children dying of hunger and disease in some remote part of the world. He must stop crying as he was aware of the eyes of one of the priests constantly looking in his direction. It was embarrassing, but still he cried.

Chapter 6

If only she had seen then what she saw now. He was rough around the edges and acted tough yet, this dark, burly man still loved her. In his heart of hearts, she had still, after all that, been the only woman of his life. She could see now that he had loved her now as much as he had when he had promised that he would love her and hold her for better or for worse, in sickness and in health, through prosperity and poverty for better and for worse until death do they part. It cut through her to the quick the pain she had caused him. But, he had caused her pain too, she thought with quiet indignation. Now, he sits looking all holy and bereaved. Shedding those tears for him or for her? She remembered how he had never let her forget what she had done to him, as if she needed reminding! The fool, didn't he realise she punished herself much more effectively than any priest, lay person, or husband could ever punish her? The fool, didn't he see that she had hated herself for what she had done more than he could ever hate her? But, then maybe that was her downfall. She wouldn't forgive herself. She wouldn't accept God's forgiveness. So, not forgiving herself or accepting her loving Master's forgiveness, how on earth was she ever going to accept his forgiveness tainted with so much pain, hurt, and misery? He had tried. Yet, that mental image had accompanied him through thick and thin, highs and lows, work and rest, and had never left him faithfully torturing him, so that when forgiveness seemed so close at hand, it would gently slip through his fingers and elude him.

Anyway, it was a clean sheet now, and this is when she will have to forgive herself and realise that all guilt is such wasted emotion and waste of energy. The guilt. It had never left her. She would not let it go. How dare she, anyway? It was the constant reminder of her unfaithfulness, yet it faithfully accompanied her day and night. Many people had wanted to help her carry it, but they didn't know how and she wouldn't let them anyway. Other people wanted her to get rid of it to ditch it and put it down leave it somewhere behind her but she couldn't. She had clung to it as if the very essence of her very existence had depended upon it, as if without it, she would die. As if now she defined who she was not through her goodness but through her sin. Strangely she thought, as much as she had perceived her sin as her downfall it wasn't. What had it been then, that brought about her downfall?

If it weren't the sin itself, what was it? She wondered. She looked closely, and it faintly began to dawn on her that it may have been the inability to let it go. How does one just let it go, just drop it, just like that? How does one suddenly stop blaming themselves, stop being angry at themselves, stop hating themselves for what they have done? Is it a decision that they make? Consciously, unconsciously? And if so, how and what tools help them do this? Aha . . . She recalled the times that her little Marie had over the years reiterated that she should forgive herself as He had forgiven her, the onus being on her, Amy. It was no use waiting for someone else to procure that forgiveness for her—it was something she would have to do herself. Only Amy could do it for herself; nobody could do it for her.

Now here in this state of being, she was beginning to become overcome by a slightly increasing sense of despair, the sense that there was no escape from here. The firm belief that she would go to a better place, for want of a better concept to pastures green in a land in which milk and honey would flow where there was no suffering, no guilt, no constant reminders of what she had done began to fade. Here, all she could do was wait and watch and begin to see how many lives she had damaged.

Why were all these thoughts coming to her here anyway? Where were the milk and honey, balm to her body and soul? Well, her body didn't need milk and honey in that box, on the aisle in the middle of the church. And as to her soul it yearned for respite from this constant thinking, over thinking, analysing and over-analysing it yearned for rest, yes, maybe in pastures green. Anyway, why hadn't He come to judge her yet? Ah, maybe he would wait until the church service was over and she was put six feet down under.

Every morning as she slowly and deliberately opened her eyes, she would curse the daylight. She would be able to see nothing else, but her pain which she would nurse like a sick child. It was as if there was no end to this pain and suffering. It was as if she would make an effort and try and get through a door . . . feel relief . . . respite . . . hope. And then, six feet further she is faced with another door . . . and then another door . . . it was a long, never-ending corridor of doors and no matter how she tried she would always end up facing a closed door . . . there was no end. She had tried originally, made a huge effort to get out of this self-centred painful way of life but, as going through one door just led to another, and another all the same with no end in sight, hope began to give way to despair and the love of life she tried to rekindle within her began to fade before it even were given a chance to shine.

At other times, she would catch a glimpse of the pain she caused others, mainly to her Marie. She would catch a glimpse of the anguish and fear in her eyes and would wonder if they would all be much happier without her. Marie would be relieved, and why wouldn't she? Ever since a child of six, Marie had felt responsible for Amy's well-being providing her with reassurance, company, and love—lots and lots of love that Amy had so desperately needed. And what did Amy give her back in return? What? Not much. She looked at Marie with both pity and compassion now. It was too late now to feel concern about how Marie had been feeling all through her life now as she walked down the altar after having finished the Reading. It was even harder for Amy to make out what her eldest daughter, the daughter she bore at barely eighteen—and not out of love as she had always explained to make sure that Marie got that loud and clear, not out of love—was feeling!

My goodness, she was confident and clear and managed those lovely words of farewell and thanking the congregation for their support that day. She could never see her, blinded by her pain she couldn't see the beauty any kind of beauty that would stare her in the face. But, now she saw her as clear as daylight. All the things she had aspired to, dreamt of, wanted in life had eluded her but seemed to be handed over to Marie instead. It was hard to watch. Why had life favoured Marie so well and had left Amy barren and stark naked with nothing left to give but pain, self-pity, and sorrow? Life. Life was really unfair. But look at her. How young and beautiful she was. What was that she detected now? A tinge of envy maybe? No. A full-blown bout of jealousy came over her, and not being embodied, she could only recognise this emotion because it was so familiar. Utterly and totally familiar. She had felt this many, many times before. She had tried to hide it hoping that her eldest daughter would never catch her out, hoping that her eldest daughter would not realise how jealous she had been of her. Of what exactly? Of everything. It did really seem to Amy at that time, the time when she had inhabited a human body, of course, that she was extremely jealous of her eldest daughter of her youth and carefree manner, her vivaciousness, her honesty, her fearlessness, her vitality, her opportunity to go to Uni, her standing in the local community, her friends, her travels, her clothes, her hair, her smile, and the list went on and on and on and could go on and on—forever.

Forever is what she had a lot of at the moment, she gently reminded herself. She would have to revisit this theme she was sure, but now her head began to hurt—well, there was a hurting sensation in space, in a space where she envisaged her head would have been, had she had a body.

It seemed like Marie had had everything she had either missed out on or didn't or couldn't have. There was one thing she didn't envy her, however. It was this one thing that she tried to warn Marie about, but Marie was either too proud, too deeply in love, or too much of a fool to listen to her. That man! He wasn't right for her. She knew. She knew all right. She had felt it in her heart and in her gut—call it a mother's intuition, maybe. She didn't know how she knew, but she knew. It was little things which convinced her that he would never be able to love her Marie in the way that she wanted and needed to be loved. This man might provide for materially but would drain her emotionally and leave her starving spiritually. He had nothing about him no spark, no initiative, no go get it! Apathy—that was it—it summed him up. Apathetic. Very brainy, clever, and academically gifted but lacking motivation, energy, and life, whereas she beamed with God's grace. He would suck it off her like a leech leaving her parched and dry taking and not giving anything back in return for sadly, he had nothing to give. Maybe, he loved her in his own quirky, selfish way but, this wasn't the man who would fulfil her daughter's need for unconditional love and deep understanding of who she is and how to help her come to wholeness.

And what about passion? Passion was something her daughter had possessed in abundance. She was passionate about her job, about the children in the deprived area where she did voluntary work locally and abroad, about the young people in the parish for whom she helped run a youth club, about travelling, about her spirituality. Basically, her Marie was in love with life and passionate about most aspects of it. She didn't do things by half measures. If she put her mind to something, she would see it through and see it through properly. Wasn't it her who had taught her that if a job was worth doing, it was worth doing well? And Marie had taken that advice to heart to guide her through her various projects and dreams in life helping her grow in confidence and earn the respect of all those around her.

He, on the other hand, seemed to lack any passion of any kind. He didn't seem passionate about Marie, either. He didn't seem too bothered whether he saw her or not during the week or over Christmas or at weekends. He seemed so withdrawn in his own little world locked in his own thoughts living life not from his heart, not from his gut, but totally and entirely from his head. If only she could get into his head at least to ascertain whether he loved her Marie or not. His heart, through a lack of use, had become frozen and unable to express any emotion and to translate through his body what his heart had felt. Frozen. Did Marie think that she would be the woman to thaw his heart for him? The one who would save him from himself and his coldness? That she would wrap him up nice and warm with her own warmth and love and that would thaw his heart and make it whole? Had she hoped she would be the one who would wake him up with a kiss as if in a fairy tale where she would kiss him and he would wake up from a seven-year slumber imposed on him, this time round not by an evil witch, but by his own doing, his own lack of trust in himself, in her and in the world. Not being able to be true to himself and true to Marie, he would bring them both down in the end.

Marie seemed happy enough, of course. But at twenty and not having had any previous boyfriends, she had nothing and nobody to compare him to, whereas, Amy had known love and passion. She had been embraced with desire, gazed upon with passion, and enveloped in love—or was it lust? It was getting a bit confusing by now, a bit of a blur. Anyway, back to the subject that had been playing heavy on her heart. She had suffered a lot when it came to the matters of the heart and wanted to spare her daughter that same pain at all costs. This detached, seemingly emotionless man wasn't going to embrace her daughter with passion, kiss her lips with lust, and envelop her in a love which would make her feel complete, cared for, and utterly and totally protected. Even if he could do it in his head, he would not be able to follow it through with his heart and with his body, with wild words of passion, whispers of lust, and the romance which normally accompanied fresh, young love. He would be able to provide, to procreate, and to progress in his career, but what else would he provide for her daughter's lust for life and zest for excitement and romance and fun? Wasn't being young and in love meant to be fun and exciting after all? Why did he think that life had to be so serious at only eighteen? Why wouldn't he ever smile? There was a sadness, a bit like a sense of having been cheated out life, about him that had bothered her from day one. She couldn't put her finger on it but often wondered if he had been torn between his Marie and some other girl. Or many other girls, maybe? Pulled him in this and that direction leaving him confused and angry at himself for needing so much yet giving so little!

It had crossed her mind many, many times whether she had chosen that day out of all the days in the year for this very reason. It didn't bear thinking about, but at this stage, as her eyes opened and there was no sleep and respite, she was faced with the stark reality of one very important trigger for her decision to end her life that day. That day in particular. This man was going to be engaged to her lovely Marie—that free-spirited girl, whom no man should capture to keep for himself. He would smother her, and slowly, little by little, he would suck all the life out of her to feed his lack of energy and lack of enthusiasm and lack of passion and lack of zest for life and lack of emotion and lack of initiative and lack of drive and motivation and lack of love that she would be bone dry with nothing left to give. It would destroy her. He would destroy her. She would never feel passion and love in the way she had as illicit as it may have been, it was passion and love nonetheless. Although, she paid for it for the rest of her life in many ways, it had been worth it. Her daughter would never know these things and that would be a huge shame.

She often had wondered and was wondering now as she listened to the Psalm they had chosen—oh not that one. That had been her long-time favourite. Of course, Psalm 23. It must have been Marie's doing. She knew her much more than she knew herself and had loved her much more than she had ever loved herself. She couldn't see any pastures green yet, and as for resting she was losing hope of that too. What happens when you despair in the afterlife? To despair in physical life, you do something to separate your body from your soul and free yourself from your life as you know it. Then the pain would go away. That she had done. Step 1 accomplished. But, the Catechism book she had read numerous times on the toilet over the years hadn't covered this specific topic and hadn't answered this very question: what happens when people despair after being separated from their bodies in the afterlife? What do they do then? The body's gone, and there is no body to torture. So what was being tortured now and for how long? A tricky question. She would have to wait and see. All this waiting and seeing was really doing her head in and getting to her. Where was the Anafranil when she needed it? Was it twelve or fourteen she had been on in the last year? How much did it take to make her sleep all day and all night to numb the throbbing pain of the questions upon questions that incessantly plagued her mind? And yet, the more she had tried to numb the pain, the brain, the questions seemed to press further and further into the front of her brain, screaming louder and louder for attention driving her insane. Hang on, this wasn't hell, was it? She knew this state of being on Earth. Why haven't all these thoughts stopped now, faded, dissipated, and disappeared? Why hadn't anything changed apart from going to being embodied to being disembodied?

She noticed that the priest stood up and calmly and deliberately walked across the altar to begin the farewell discourse. Why this priest? Would he know to mention the hours she had spent scrubbing and cleaning the church floor? Would he remember to mention that she had gone to Mass on average twice a day in the last few years and she had sat devoutly in one of the front seats reserved for her? Would this priest know how many times she had prayed the Rosary every day? How devout she had been? How she had loved St Francis of Assisi and avidly read his life story over and over again? Gone to Medjugorje on a pilgrimage with her daughter and son? Would he know that she had fasted three days a week and ate bland cereal on most days to atone for her sins?

It hadn't been that she had particularly loved cleaning the pews, the floors, the chandeliers, and the candlesticks. It was more that in cleaning the church, she had hoped she would cleanse her soul of its sins, of its iniquities! She had hoped that this would be a penance that would purge her of her sins and grant her heavenly forgiveness. There was one thing that neither this particular priest nor any other for that matter would know—only Marie had ever been told and it was only because it had concerned her directly. Anyway, surely he wouldn't mention it in front of the whole congregation if he knew anyway, would he? Everybody had at some point thought she had actually really been mad, and this would have confirmed it to many.

However, she recalled as bright as day that night when Marie barely eight years old came to wake her up in the middle of the night saying that there was a man who had wanted to speak with her. That this man was called Jesus. She perched herself up to sit in her bed and indeed, there at the bottom of her bed was the plainest Jesus she had ever seen. No fancy beard, dark, beady eyed, and very plain. He told her that her sins had all been forgiven. She did not need to suffer any more for her sins. She did not have to voluntary endure hardship for her sins. She did not need to continue to punish herself for her sins as they have been forgiven! He had already paid for them on the cross, anyway. She had been repentant, and this she knew and accepted her repentance. Then he left as swiftly has she had appeared. Marie had gone back to bed, and when asked the next morning if she remembered the incident from the previous night, she maintained that she hadn't. And she hadn't. Marie didn't lie, and if she said she didn't recall getting up and waking her mum up in the middle of the night and telling her that Jesus wanted a word, then she didn't! But, that didn't stop her from believing her mum's words and thinking that her mum in her weird, quirky way may have been a saint—with a past. If only, she would be able to forgive, love, and embrace herself, Marie had wondered over the years, then all of the tragedies that followed would have been avoided. That's all that had been necessary, Marie was convinced. And Marie was convinced that this is still the main source of misery in the world—if people would only embrace their humanity and accept themselves lovingly for who they are, giving themselves the love that they so yearn for, and able to accept it from others who offer it, then many people would make themselves whole again. Simple.

Will she forgive herself now? Will she? Oh, saved by the bell, as they say! The bell to signify it was time for consecration of the bread and wine. She was never as relieved as this to hear this bell go and the little prayer that went with it. She couldn't kneel today, of course, but that was OK; it was a distraction which was so welcomed. All this thinking and asking was making her ill. But, hadn't she allegedly been mentally ill since twenty-three? She would have to think a bit more about this one—a heavy one—this one. One topic which she had tried not to think about in her previous life, but why does it keep coming back? Oh bother!

Her train of thoughts were happily interrupted by Holy Communion. How odd to watch every single person go up to receive the bread and not to be one of them. Just three days earlier, she had been there, on that very same bench, walking up the very same aisle and taking the bread with everyone else. Every day without fail she would. Sometimes, even twice a day. How grateful she had been for the new decree that the Pope had issued a few years earlier stating that you could receive Communion twice a day. Not once, but twice a day! And by Jove did she make the most of it. She had longed for her soul to be purified and purged of the evil she had committed in her youth, and she was sure that scrubbing the church floors, polishing the brass and silverware, and taking communion twice a day would do it. Of course, giving money to charity and helping individual members of the priesthood have a comfortable life had also been included in this long list by which she would procure her own salvation. It felt so strange that now having no body, she can eat no bread and drink no wine at communion. And now as she watched, she wondered why her soul didn't feel pure and why she was being plagued by doubt, fear, shame, and guilt. Where was He anyway? Hadn't He promised to come and greet her and tell her if she were worthy of His kingdom or not? Maybe she hadn't purged herself after all. Maybe she had gone about it the wrong way? Marie had had other ideas of how she could purge herself and forgiving and loving and embracing herself had been Marie's top tips. She hadn't believed that something so simply stated could have been the answer and could have saved her. Forgive herself just like that. It was much easier said than done. She was adamant that the answer lay in rituals and ceremonies out there—not within herself and within the power she had within her to forgive herself. Anyway, time was pressing, and He still hadn't appeared. Where was He? Indisposed? Otherwise engaged? Busy, perhaps?! Understandable, of course, as she hadn't been scheduled to see him until about another twenty or thirty or even forty years later.

This wasn't going at all as she had expected. Having taken the law into her own hands, she honestly believed she should be, on His priority list—an unexpected guest, a visitor, who should be treated as a matter of urgency and not made to so rudely wait. When would He next be free to see her? He wasn't into playing games, was He? It was all true what He had preached, was it? In my Father's house, there are many rooms, and I will go and I will prepare you a room, so that where I am so you will be also! But, for heaven's sake, where was He now? Here she was. Of that there was no doubt, but where was He so that she could be there also with Him as she had yearned for at least the last twenty years? It was partly His fault for making His Father's kingdom seem so perfect—a perfect state of peace, tranquillity, safety—where no harm would come to anybody. It was madness waiting for another twenty years when she could have it now! Her strong faith which together with the love of her Marie had carried her through life for the last twenty years was beginning to waver, when suddenly she felt a jolt. 'He must be coming,' she thought with relief.

However, to her utter and total disappointment, it was only the coffin being lifted up by several men including her beloved Matt and Mike to be taken into the back of the funeral car which would take her corpse to be buried at a cemetery on the other side of the island. These had been the longest three days she had ever known. She cracked, it! Of course, three days, that's it. Her waiting would be over now, and she would see Him as three days is how many days he had waited for, and hence it would be how long she would have to wait for. Hurray, all this waiting would soon come to an end! As soon as her lifeless body hit the bottom of the tailor-made hole, her waiting would be over and He would appear. Wow, will she be pleased to see Him! She couldn't wait.

Chapter 7

She couldn't help but wonder if he would be wearing a long white robe, a bushy brown beard, and a shepherd's staff in his hand. As her body was being lowered into the grave, she was so relieved! Not that at this point in time it mattered whether it was in a coffin, in a grave, in the middle of the ocean, in a dump, in a furnace being burnt to smithereens, to be honest. The relief came from the fact that now that her body was being lowered, it had been three days after it all had happened—He would appear. This wasn't a hope, an expectation as it had been previously. No, this was sheer certainty—He would appear to her as He had done to Mary Magdalene on the third day. Hurray! This nightmare would soon come to an end and she would be free, free from the pain of this sense of shame that had suddenly taken over her disembodied being, this seeing the things she hadn't wanted to see, perceiving now more than ever before that her actions had had an impact possibly irreversible on all the people she had claimed to have loved in her lifetime. Her shame was beginning to feel a bit like remorse.

The social dimension of sin had been one thing she had always struggled with in the past. If one decided to top themselves and put an end to it all as they'd had enough, surely others should understand. Surely, if they had loved her dearly, they would want for her what she had so fervently yearned for herself for so many years of her adult life. Surely, they will not judge and condemn her. Now, she would say that they would not judge and condemn her—not as much as she had been judging and condemning herself in the last seventy-two hours! She remembered His words: 'Has nobody condemned you woman, if not, then neither will I. Go on your way and sin no more.' Why had she been so keen to take on the words he had spoken of condemnation (Alas for you, you Pharisees . . .), but not the ones in which he had described his Father's Love, his Father's infinite capacity for forgiveness, His own capacity for inwardly healing and making whole, for wanting everybody to be healed so that they can love as He loves and forgive as He forgives. It's funny that, isn't it? She did it all the time she only took on board what suited her, but mostly what confirmed her state as an unredeemable sinner as if she had wanted to continue to punish herself, when He, Marie, and possibly Mike had all been trying to forgive her. Again, she got the feeling that she had defined herself through this pain, and this had made her who she was. She wouldn't know what to do with herself if she had actually had the courage to free herself of the guilt, anger, and fear that assaulted her. She held onto them, clinging to them as if they were her best allies, her friends. Little did she realise that the more she clung to this suffering, the tighter her fists became in not letting go, the tighter the noose around her neck became, the harder to breathe freely, to move freely, to talk freely and to act freely. This would be what would classify her in the medical world as mentally ill. In the spiritual realm, it would be translated as an inability, an unwillingness to let go, to define herself through her suffering and pain, rather than through the utter and total perfection that God had intended for each and every one of his creatures—His beloved creation. The urge to suffer was so great, the urge to perpetuate the suffering was even greater. Hadn't her Master suffered? Wasn't that what she had been meant to emulate? How had the message in her head become so skewed? Why hadn't she realised that although he had suffered, he had risen after the third day overcoming suffering and pain? Whereas her suffering led her to despair, His led to everlasting life. Where and how did she get it all so muddled up?

It hadn't been like that all her life. She had lovely childhood memories being brought up in that suburban town. One story she always liked to tell Marie was of how when she had been little, she had been all dressed up to go to a party. She had looked absolutely gorgeous in her brand new dress, shoes, and head band. However, whilst waiting for everyone else to get ready, she kept herself amused by watching the frogs in the pond at the end of their garden. Her dad hadn't had much time to waste on digging ponds for frogs—it has to be said—but since Amy had been born after three boys, he had made an effort, and in order to keep her amused and entertained, he dug a hole, covered it up with canvas, sealed the edges, filled it with water, and lo and behold, there it was—a pond. A pond with lots of happy frogs croaking and frogging about. She felt a bit envious of their freedom to croak when they pleased, jump when they fancied, and eat and drink at will and decided she wanted a taste of what their life was like. So, suddenly, intrigued by their lifestyle, she threw herself deep in the pond thinking that by being in there and partaking in their lifestyle, she too could be a bit of a rebel and gain some freedom. Freedom? Freedom from what? Whilst her eldest brother ousted her out of there, she heard her mum screaming at her saying she was grounded. She had never made it to the party. Her new shoes had been ruined, her dress, her hair. Maybe, this had been a foreboding of what lay ahead—the pattern that her life would follow. Other people would jump into ponds, fall into rivers, fall flat on their bellies, and everyone else would act as if they hadn't put a foot wrong—they wouldn't be judged or thought any less of. Moreover, it didn't seem to come back to bite them with a vengeance. Why was it so different with her? Why was it that every time she set a foot wrong, there would be a consequence? And not any consequence, a serious consequence which seemed much out of proportion to the magnitude of the crime. Lots of people had affairs with their bosses, with their co-workers, with their neighbours, with their friend's boyfriends, with the milkman, postman, you name it, it's being done. Nothing new under the sun. She had a two-year love affair with her husband's best friend, and alas, all hell breaks loose and the consequences follow her to her grave—and beyond!

First, there were the twins. Matthew and Gloria. Why had he promised her that he would leave his wife for her if he then went and got her pregnant at the same time? Two women, his wife and his illicit lover pregnant at the same time. Would she have ever told Mike if he hadn't found her and Gary out that they weren't his? Would she have ever told him that these twins were actually conceived by an act of love? Not an act of dutiful sex, not an act of being stroked and caressed by a man she had no feelings for, who she loved and cared for as a friend, a brother but not a lover.

No. These twins were conceived in an act of love with a man she was madly in love with, counting the hours until their next encounter, their next embrace, the next kiss, the next time she would lay her head on his strong, comforting, reassuring chest. And, having been conceived out of love, they did not survive. How was it that anything good that had ever happened to her in life had been marred in some way or another? If it were bad, it stayed; if it were good, it died?! Why was that? Was it that she believed she didn't deserve good things to happen to her? Or maybe, she was jinxed from birth? Or cursed even? Maybe her conception wasn't one that emerged out of a loving encounter—but, that she would never get to know.

In a way, it was a blessing in disguise that she had miscarried them at six months. But she never recovered from that tragedy. Never. That scene had stayed with her, to haunt her and daunt her for the rest of her days. For the next twenty years after that, she would not find peace, reconciliation, and forgiveness, and her life would be like that of a nomad searching for a homeland to rest their head for the night, but no matter how long she travelled for, that land never appeared and her head never rested. It was an accident. Chasing after the lambs that had escaped from the allotment at six months pregnant shouldn't have caused a miscarriage. But she tripped over, fell, and nearly bled to death killing the twins in her womb. Still born. Hospital. Little white coffins. Church. Graveyard. She had gone through the whole process as if in a sleepwalking-like state and continued in this state for the rest of her life hoping she would never be woken up. She blamed herself for an accident that was meant to happen, an accident which Fate or Destiny or The Will of God or Life had decreed. And she wouldn't forgive herself for this, ever. Well, not until she had died anyway.

She had hoped that her head would rest now. Well, in actual fact, it was. Buried under six feet of dirt, her head did not have to move or do anything really. So, where were all these thoughts stemming from? If her head were buried six feet under, her brain cells were already turning to mush, and the nerve endings that connected the spine to the brain as dead as a dodo, then were where these incessant, annoying thoughts coming from? Where were these feelings emerging from? What was going on? Why hadn't she stopped thinking? She couldn't stop obsessing when she had been in a body, but how was she doing it now? Surely, the main reason she did what she did was to silence the incessant voices in her head which wouldn't allow her a moment's peace. Nothing could shut those thoughts up. Nothing. Apart from the tranquillisers, of course. They not only numbed her brain, but also her body. The state of sleepwalking perpetuated.

Yet, the thoughts still came and with the same fury and the same frequency—incessant. Maybe not with the same level of loudness. Taking the drugs was like putting the sound down. Making them slightly fainter, slightly as if in the distance, that's all. Simple. But, then that didn't last for long and the dose had to be increased regularly. Increasing the dose worked as it meant that she spent a lot of the daytime sleeping. Sleeping was like balm to her spirit. Sleeping was when she was well and truly at peace. That was the only time she would stop thinking. But, as soon as she opened her eyes—lo and behold—they would be back—sometimes in the shape of fearful demons and sometimes as elusive ghosts. Sometimes, screaming and shouting, sometimes like a gentle whisper in the distance. But these thoughts, they came, nonetheless, as soon as she opened her eyes after every one of her long-drawn sleeps. If only she had realised then, that it wasn't the seeing that was the trouble and hearing of the thoughts it was the self-condemnation she attached to them, the constant self-judging that accompanied them, and the shame and guilt that they were shrouded in.

Her hope had been that ending it all meant eternal rest which to her meant eternal sleep. Now, shocked to the core, it is beginning to dawn on her that it's an eternal state of being awake. How will she cope? Everybody had left the cemetery by now, and she could tell it was getting late. One by one, they had trickled away. Her mum, her dad, her husband, her daughter, her son, her mother-in-law, her father-in-law, her brothers and sisters-in-law, cousins, aunts, and uncles were also dispersing until the cemetery was only inhabited by ghosts like her.

And He hadn't made an appearance yet. So not only was she left waiting, but she was left waiting awake. If only she could shut her eyes and sleep for a short while, that would be great, but it seemed very unlikely that that would happen at this stage. A sense of despair deeper than the one that had made her commit suicide overcame her, and she began to sob gently until her sobbing turned into crying until her crying turned into a wailing, at least there was no gnashing of teeth as she didn't have any now. She can't have gone to hell—that she knew—she had atoned for her sins and punished herself like no God in his good senses would punish her. So where on earth was He, what was she doing there, and when were these two questions going to be answered?

Chapter 8

She didn't know how long she had been waiting for now. To begin with, she knew as she followed the funeral and burial ritual and knew that it had all happened within three days—the three longest days of her existence. But, now it seemed as if all the time was blurring into one and she couldn't quite tell what day it was and how long she had been waiting for. There was one person who would help her with that, and that was her Marie.

Marie had always been there for her when she had still inhabited a body. Marie had been patient with her. Very patient. Always reassuring. Stubborn like herself, but very kind and generous, nonetheless. Young and beautiful and full of life. Look at her, how does she do it? Anyway, she noticed that her thoughts kept drifting just like they had done in her previous existence. Time. She had been thinking about the passage of time and how she would be able to tell how long she had been waiting and knew that as soon as Marie tied the knot in this unfortunate union with this melancholic man, she, Amy, would have been waiting for six months. Six months. Six months is a long time even when you're busy and you don't stop. Six months is a longer time she thought when you have nothing to do, but to think and think and think until you begin to ache all over. She wasn't sure which part of her being hurt, unlike when you have a body and could easily locate a pain somewhere, now it was quite hard, nearly impossible to tell in which part of her spirit that pain resided. It felt like it had been everywhere as if every inch of her being ached a pain similar to that of when in labour.

Marie, like always, would be her lifeline. Before Marie had endured a lot of suffering inflicted upon her by Amy but supported her throughout and never stopped loving her, nonetheless. Now she would suffer no more but would support her still. But, how did Amy know that Marie would suffer no more? That is what she had hoped. She had convinced herself that Marie would be much better off without her and that's what she had kept telling herself now. But, did she have any way of really knowing?

The grace of this place and state of being seemed to be that she could tell if and how much a person were suffering, especially if it had been pain caused by her words or actions in the past. Well, it wasn't a grace really as much as a pain. An unbearable pain. An anguish. As if now her and the person she had caused pain to were one and that the pain she had caused she herself felt in its full force. The suffering she had inflicted on others she could feel as it were being inflicted now upon her very own self. How is it possible that she had never been able to perceive the impact of her behaviour before? She had hoped that she would be excused from her behaviour as she had always been up to now. But here, there was no escape—no excuse was valid and no label would do to absolve her of her hard headedness, pride, and unwillingness to see and hear or of her ignorance.

The shrivelling of her inner world, the tightness of her heart, the brokenness which had caused her to shut down and protect herself—unable to love herself or anyone else—were there with her as large as life. The acts of love she had performed were always through such an effort—everything in the daytime living world had been an effort—if she remembered correctly. Maybe, not church cleaning and praying. But apart from that, preparing meals, cleaning the house, ironing their clothes, shopping, and having sex were all chores which required a tremendous amount of effort. Marie had always known this as Amy hadn't kept this fact a secret from her. She would understand. But, in actual fact, Marie hadn't understood and didn't understand. In Marie's world, love, true love, was effortless and spontaneous—something that came flowing from the heart. Spilling over and filling everywhere with a joy, laughter, and fun. No. She didn't understand. Watching her mother plod on day after day making such a massive effort to get out of bed, to get through the day and be grateful for the night and the long, long afternoon siestas had caused her a lot of pain. Amy could see this now, and she didn't like what she could see. Marie had cared. Marie had loved her. Marie had tried in every way possible to help her carry her pain wishing it upon herself many more times than Amy could have imagined. Marie woke up every day with the hope that her mother would be better today, happier and feeling OK with life. On the days when Amy did perk up, Marie's face would light up and with a huge sigh of relief would smile to herself in the mirror and reassure herself that life wasn't that painful after all and that all would be well.

Now, on the other hand, Marie detested anyone who would use the cliché 'All will be well . . . all manner of things will be well . . .' How dare they assume? They hadn't lived through the pain she had—and no, it hadn't all ended well and all manner of things hadn't been well, were not well, and wouldn't be well for many, many years to come. What a liberty! What a f**king liberty!

Amy could detect the anger, possibly rage, underlying Marie's strong reaction to that cliché and wondered whether this was there due to the pain she herself had caused Marie. There was a lot of anger, hurt, and a feeling of rejection. But hadn't she understood? In all those years, didn't she know that the only thing she had wanted to do during life was to die?

Marie knew only too well. To have lived with a mother who detested a 'good morning' meant that she hadn't been taken away during the night caused pain in itself. Then Amy would reiterate to Marie that the only reason she was still there was because she had wanted to make Marie's life easier. If Amy were gone, Marie would have to cook, clean, wash, shop, iron, and that would have stopped her getting a good education, going to Uni, and landing a fulfilling career in teaching. She wasn't that selfish. However, she had made sure that Marie knew of this massive sacrifice, this act of selfless love that Amy was making for Marie. And Marie knew, undoubtedly. There was not one day that she had not been reminded of this fact. Day in and day out, her mother would reassure her that she would wait till she finished secondary school, then till she finished sixth form, and then till she finished her degree at university. Of course, she couldn't bear to attend the graduation, but at least she had hung around long enough for her daughter to make it in the world and have a profession—a chance much bigger than any she had ever been given. It was only because Amy couldn't bear to see her daughter get married and possibly be as unhappy as she had been for the rest of her life that gave her the impetus to do what she did. As for Marie, the threat that had been hanging over her head for the last twenty years was now suddenly a reality.

Marie had had to live with this state of constant uncertainty and insecurity throughout her childhood, teenage, and adult years. She would go home after school, after work, after a day out, and wonder if her mum would be there on her return. If she weren't, then it would be because she would have left her dad or decided to end it all. One day, Marie clearly recalled being physically sick with worry at the prospect of getting home after school not to find her mother there. She waited and waited, her body frozen with fear and her mind numb with terror at the prospect that the day had come when her mum had just upped and left or worse still had ended it all. She remembered the sigh of relief tinged with irritation and anger when the door opened and her mother all cheery and happy waltzed through with a bag full of freshly cut meat from the local butchers. And at thirteen, this was the tip of the iceberg as much worse was in store for this girl at the beginning of her teenage years. Her patience, love, fortitude, inner strength, and courage would be tried and tested beyond belief and she would come out the other end one day, one day in the long distant future she would. If only she knew that at the time.

She would lay her head on her freshly laundered pillow at night, as her mum had been a meticulous cleaner and an amazing cook, and pray to her God that she would not ever end up like her mother. She went to bed every night terrified that as she grew older, she too would go insane, get depressed, and being unable to cope with life, curse every dawning of the new day and bless every evening as the sun set, signifying the end of a long day bringing with it not just the end of a day, but hopefully the end of an era, an end to a life. She didn't know who to turn to. Life was terribly lonely, and she was scared, very scared.

At that time, there was nobody to talk to. Her brother Matthew had been too young, her father Mike too busy, too rough, and too angry, and her mother Amy too self-absorbed, too resentful, and too depressed. She would confide in her grandma who had loved Marie with unconditional love since she had been born and separated for many years, reunited in body and in love once again on the island after many years.

They say that life is like a box of chocolates—you never know what you're gonna get! What if she got the same lot in life as her mum? She began to wonder as she lay her head on her pillow for the night. What would she do then? She had felt responsible for the welfare and well-being of her beloved mother since she had been six years old. The role reversal had happened one late afternoon when she had found her mum in a heap on the floor crying her eyes out. She did not know then, but that was the moment, she was to find out many years later in therapy with a holy Benedinctine monk when she, Marie, had taken on the role of mother caring for the woman who had brought her into this world six years earlier at barely eighteen.

Amy remembered that day clearly. She hadn't wanted her little innocent, happy daughter for whom she had devoted her life to and who had been the centre of her universe to see her in that state. First came gentle sobbing, then crying followed by loud wailing and it was as if she couldn't stop. She remembered Marie's tiny hands resting on her back and patting her back, trying to soothe her by rubbing it. She knew even at six not to use any words to comfort—a gentle laying of hands would be enough. Amy had felt so reassured and comforted by this heartfelt gesture of love from her loving and doting daughter, but it made her cry even more as she realised how unable to take care of this vulnerable child she had been and how it was unnatural for a daughter to comfort the mother at such an early age. She, Amy, had brought this innocent, beautiful child into the world to love and cherish and love and cherish she did try but, now it was this little girl's lot in life to love and cherish her own mother, not as a daughter but as a mother to love and protect. But who would protect her?

Marie loved Grandma Jo and sometimes did confine in her, but Grandma Jo was her mother's mother and she didn't want to bother her with her own daughter's iniquities. Grandma Jo only got to know about Amy's affair years after it had happened and had disowned her daughter for many years. That afternoon when Amy had been like a pile on the floor crying her eyes out being comforted by Marie had been brought about precisely by the news that her own mother had disowned her. Grandma Jo firmly blamed her daughter for leaving the land Down Under and going back to the island as it had divided the family between the two hemispheres separating Grandma Jo from her most treasured youngest son still in the land Down Under young and having to fend for himself. For this, she blamed Amy. She had to follow Amy back to the Island of their origin—a land she had hoped to have left for good to follow and support Amy and Amy's older brother who had followed suit to be with Marie. To cut a long story short, things between the two women had never been the same after that. Grandma Jo had tried to love her daughter, but something inside her had stunted her motherly love, she didn't know quite what. It's not that she hadn't loved her daughter. She had loved her daughter. But her daughter had shut her out. At seventeen, she had decided to marry a man she did not love to get rid of her authoritarian dad and had never breathed a word about it to Grandma Jo. When years later Grandma Jo had learnt of the affair and how Amy had married Mike not out of love but out of a desperate need to get away from her dad, she had felt betrayed. Betrayed by the fact that her daughter hadn't loved her and hadn't trusted her enough to confide in her. Why hadn't her daughter turned to her for help? She had found it hard to forgive her for that. She had found it hard to forgive her for having broken the family up between two continents, breaking Grandma Jo's heart in half. She had also found it hard to forgive her for how she had always treated that precious little angel whose heart was so pure and whose soul sang of love, who filled her world with joy and made her heart glow with joy, her little Marie.

But who would protect Marie? Who indeed? A good question. Amy often wondered that too. Who would protect her little one if she couldn't? Mike? Well, Mike needed taking care of and protecting himself. He was still injured and inwardly utterly broken. Shaken and misshapen. He and Amy had decided to have another child years after that. Another innocent child brought into a loveless marriage to hopefully save the marriage?

Amy, as she was looking back now, did wonder why people still bought into this fallacy. Quit while you're ahead she would say to them now, but for Heaven's sake do not bring another innocent life into this world with the hope that it will solve your relationship problems because it won't. And for Amy and Mike, it didn't. In fact, it made it much worse. Mike resented all the love and attention that Amy had lavished on this angelic being of a blond baby who looked like a little Cupid who would make your heart burst with love. Now, Marie would be so happy to have a baby brother, with hazel green eyes and blond hair and a very generous and open heart. They would suffer a lot together, and as for Marie, instead of just taking care of her mother, she had to nurture and bring up her baby brother.

What had she been thinking? What was she thinking now? Well, to begin with why was she going back in time? What was this all about? She had conceded to the fact that somehow it would have to be Marie who would show her the passage of time (why it had to be Marie? She didn't quite know, and didn't know if she'd ever find out!)—the passage of time forwards and *not* backwards. She didn't care in going backwards; she wanted to go forwards so that she could stop this waiting and waiting and unbearable waiting. She detested this state of being where she was totally and utterly powerless. She hated seeing these things now as clear as daylight and not being able to change them or do anything about them. What had been done had been done, full stop. If she couldn't change it, what was the point of dwelling on it? What was the point of dredging up all these painful memories? What was the point of all of this thinking and watching and waiting, anyway?

Going backwards wasn't going to get her anywhere. And the more she went backwards, the more powerless she felt and the more helpless she became. Powerlessness and helplessness. Helplessness and powerlessness. Hadn't that been the story of her life? Why had she revisited these themes with a vengeance in her death? Was there no end to her suffering and pain?

It now had began to dawn on her that Marie would show her the passage of time and that this was true. Marie would be the link between the two worlds—the world of the fully bodied and the world of the disembodied—but it would come at a price. She had known through bitter-sweet experience that nothing in life came for free. Everything had a price. And, if Marie were going to be this link, it would have to come at a price also.

Amy didn't want it to be that way. She had genuinely believed that not having had her own way on Earth, she would then get her own way as soon as her body was crushed to smithereens that fatal day just five days before Christmas—Eternal rest she had thought. Eternal rest in the land overflowing with milk and honey as the Old Testament said. Eternal rest where her soul already purged through church and house cleaning would soar high towards the heavens, be met by her Maker, judged kindly by Him, and cordially invited to join Him in His kingdom thereafter, forever and forever. Amen.

There would be no suffering, no pain, no painful memories, no guilt, no shame, no reprimands, no regret—only peace, peace, peace and rest, rest, rest. How wrong could she have been. Not only had He not appeared (and it was approaching the wedding now, so it must be approaching six months since she had died), but she was more alive than ever before, continuing to live through the pain she had caused those she had so claimed to have loved. Especially through Marie's pain as she had hurt her so much, sometimes intentionally and sometimes unintentionally. She had let her own unfilled wishes fill her with resentment as she saw them being fulfilled in her daughter. She would make demands for her daughter's love, attention, and time, and her daughter would kindly and lovingly oblige, with a lot of compassion and love as she cared deeply for this woman and loved her dearly, this mother of hers.

But, as she grew older, the demands grew bigger and bigger, and no matter how much Marie gave it was never enough, Amy always wanted more. And Marie would then give more and more and more until consumed by her mother's pain she didn't know where Amy ended and she herself started. After the third day of Amy's death, Marie did not have a clue who she was, what she believed in anymore, and why all the love she had lavished on Amy had been thrown back to her face in one act of defiance, of pride, of despair! It would take her years to untangle herself from this web of manipulation and emotional abuse that she had endured over the years by her mother's desperate need for love, reassurance, and acceptance. And she had hoped at that time that she would be one day able to forgive her mother, completely and utterly forgive her for smashing her world to pieces and leaving her feeling utterly helpless and totally vulnerable—and completely dead inside.

But, now Marie was unaware of her role as the one who would determine when Amy would be released from this state of utter and complete limbo. Now, Marie would be the one who would be her timekeeper, showing her how many years would have to pass before she would be able to rest. The only thing she had been told, by the Benedictine Monk at the Abbey, was that there had been a psychic link that had existed between her and her mother and that Marie would not be completely healed until that link had been severed. He would lay his hands on her, anoint her, pray with her, and although released of guilt after seven years of her mother's death, the link had not disappeared. Marie didn't know why at the time, but would find out in many years to come.

Amy, on the other hand, longed for her eyes to close and get some sleep, but respite was not on the agenda and neither were rest and peace. Not for now, and not for a very, very long time. It would have to be when Marie had totally forgiven her, and it would have to be Marie who would set her free. Marie. Her lifeline in life and in death.

Chapter 9

She woke up with a start. Finally, it seemed as if her eyes had gently shut and she was allowed some respite. Rest. She felt relieved, a renewed strength. She hoped that many years had passed with each breath as she had slumbered. Yet, it was only a few moments she had been allowed to lightly nod off. She recognised the music but not the place. She recognised the people but not the priest. She recognised the readings and the readers but not the people in the choir.

She had rather slept through Marie's wedding day if she had to be honest. But the playing of the organ was so loud it jolted her back to being fully conscious and wide awake. This respite seemed to come in very small doses, and it had seemed that when she just couldn't take anymore suffering and when what she saw had been so painful, she would be allowed to be unconscious for a short while until she regained enough inner strength to deal with the next set of painful memories or experiences.

He still hadn't appeared. It was six months and four days that she had been waiting, and it had seemed like a whole eternity. Amy had never been daunted by the idea of eternity, an eternity in His Kingdom. Not, this waiting with nothing to do and nowhere to go. This she hadn't bargained for—an eternity of waiting and watching and thinking and dissecting and judging and analysing accompanied by feelings of guilt, shame and anguish. It was draining her. She felt so tired of it all. Yet here there was no escape. When will it all end? What would she need to do now to make all of this go away? Here, all on her own, how was she going to put an end to all this? The question was more pertinent now, than it had been only three days after she had died as she felt as if she were going out of her mind.

Before, she would take pills to sleep through days and endless days of meaninglessness. And when thoughts of taking responsibility for her own actions came like thoughts of what she knew she had to do to end the pain and suffering or thoughts of what she had to change to make her reality bearable and thoughts of how to stop hurting Marie and Mike and herself she would just ask for more drugs to numb the pain of seeing, knowing, and realising. It was easier that way—then nothing had to change. It had been so effective in stunting any creative thought and any change in the status quo. The status quo, which so many people die to perpetuate even though it may be hell on Earth—how strange but, this is exactly what she herself had done. Here, there was no escape. No escape. No respite bar a few breaths of occasionally nodding off and then being brought back to the harsh realities of life—a life she had denounced about six months earlier—but, from which there seemed to be no escape now.

So, it was true. Marie was going to go ahead in spite of everything. The stubbornness of that child! Unbelievable! She was as stubborn as herself, if not more. In that respect, they had been so similar. Both standing their ground and fighting for freedom. Both standing up for what they believed was right and fair. Both very generous, hardworking, and kind. Both very stubborn and hard-headed. That's why they had always clashed so much. That's why they had antagonised each other so much. In so many ways, they had been so similar. In so many ways. Yet, in many other ways, they were poles apart. One was for life, one for death; one for joy, one for sorrow; one for forgiveness, one for self-punishment; one for self-acceptance and one for self-condemnation; one for love, one for despair; one for change, one for stagnation; one for moving forward, one for standing still; one for dancing, one for sitting; one for being awake; one for being asleep; one choosing to see; one choosing not to see; one taking responsibility, one not taking any responsibility; one for guilt one for remorse and the list went on and on and on.

Today, Amy did not feel jealous of her Marie; in fact, she pitied her. She whole-heartedly wished that because of her death, Marie would postpone or even cancel the wedding. In that way, her death would not have been totally in vain. It would have served a purpose—a very good one at that. But, that stubborn girl had always believed she could change the world. She believed she could open the heart of this man whose heart was made of steel surrounded by a brick wall that would become higher, harder, and thicker as the years went by. If only her daughter hadn't been so naïve, so trusting, so full of hope.

On the other hand, why had Marie thought that this is as much love as she would ever get from a man? The love he offered her, (and even Marie had been aware of this since the beginning of their relationship) was like breadcrumbs, leftovers falling off a lavishly laid table. Amy couldn't understand why had her daughter settled for that, when she could have freshly baked, highly risen loaves of bread? And not just bread but butter, cheese, jam, fresh fruit, biscuits, muesli and honey? Lots of young, handsome, and kind-hearted men had chased after her Marie, seeing in her the goodness that this man would try his best to eventually destroy. Lots of generous, life-loving, open-hearted men would have loved to have fallen into the arms of her Marie and she could have had a man who would truly love her, set her heart on fire, take care of her and protect her and what does she do? She gives her heart away to man who would lust after many other women. She gives her heart away to man who sees her goodness not as something to be cherished but as a threat to his own selfishness, self-centeredness, and childishness. She gives her heart and her life away to a man who needs constant reassurance of how handsome, good-looking, and intelligent he is—not from her Marie only—oh no, but from many other numerous women whom he would meet on his journey through life. It didn't even bear thinking his name, and she wouldn't mention his name in her head, that is, thoughts, not even now. She would just refer to him as The Man.

Deep down she could now see that he had wanted to be a good man. The Man had really wanted to be a good man, and he himself had hoped that

Marie would be his salvation, who would save him from himself and from his own selfishness and weakness. She would do it for him as he had seen her do with her mum. He had hoped that his need for constant validation from beautiful women would subside as they got married and he wouldn't need to have that anymore. He had hoped that the love his Marie would lavish on him would heal him, make him whole, and he wouldn't need anybody else to make him feel good about himself. He wouldn't need to feed his ego so much as her love would dissolve it. He had hoped that she would help him preserve his goodness and help him overcome or even melt away his insecurities and that she would shield him from his own pain. And in that way, he would have to do none of the work himself. He would not have to take any responsibility for any of his misdemeanours and misconduct—she would do it all for him. Perhaps, she would take full responsibility of his salvation and appear in his place when he is being judged on the day?

He had never realised that that's precisely what she had hoped for too. That had been her lifelong dream, too. She would be the one to save him from himself and from his incessant need for affirmation from any beautiful woman that happened to cross his path. And of course, in his profession, many beautiful women did cross his path many times a day. He wished he would not take advantage of his position of power, but eventually his need for affirmation grew instead of diminishing and his position of power facilitated the feeding of his hungry ego. It seemed as if over the years, his ego became greedier and greedier until it finally consumed him. That coupled with pride and arrogance was what would be the end of him, and Marie would have to live with that. He would have nothing to give her. His needs would devour him. He would only be able to take or to steal every ounce of life Marie had possessed to feed his own growing needs which were like a bottomless pit from which it would take years for him to climb out of if he ever did.

Who knows where Amy would be by then? Would she be able to help her Marie in any way? She had always told Marie that she would make a much better mother once she had 'crossed over to the other side' as she would be much closer to Him and her prayers would be answered. Her prayers to deliver her daughter from walking the same road she had walked and falling on the same stumbling blocks that she had tripped over. Her prayers would be answered if she were with Him, but He still hadn't appeared and her prayers were far from being heard. All she could do at this stage was to watch, wait, and see. That's all she had been able to do for the last six plus months. Not much help to anyone really. This was the first time she had actually regretted not being there in a physical body. Perhaps, if she had stayed in her physical body, she would have been able to actually do something practical to stop her demented daughter from forging ahead procuring her own life sentence. What would or could she have actually done?

Surely, she wouldn't have had the courage to 'accidently' stain the wedding dress? Or hide the shoes? Fake a fainting fit? Demand to be taken back to hospital on the day? Go missing and hope that they would have to spend the whole day in search for her? Speak out during the service and proclaim the unsuitability of the match? She smiled mischievously at herself as she imagined having gone for the last option. It would have been hilarious as his side of the family would have fully agreed with her. For different reasons and on different grounds, but they would have supported her. They too had thought that Marie had been unsuitable for their Man but did not dare even ever entertain the thought of saying it out loud and clear. They were of the breed which brushed things conveniently under the carpet hoping that they would go away, of course. They were of the breed that would beat about the bush, but never say it as it is—calling a spade a spade was not something they were good at.

No. Although they would have totally embraced the outburst having been caused by Amy in the church, it would have been for another reason. It would have been that the unsuitability they were concerned about was social standing. Their position in society and how they perceived it and they perceived others to perceive it. It was true that Marie had had a degree—a four-year degree at that—the same degree (the same year also) as their second daughter, but her beginnings were very humble beginnings. The daughter of a local fisherman and truck driver—what would she have to offer their Man? Why hadn't he gone for that lovely long-legged brunette whose dad had been a renowned jeweller and had been very wealthy? Or for the other brunette who lived in the same prestigious village as them in a massive villa whose father earned lots of money and whose mother always looked as if she had come out of a beauty parlour? He liked her, and she liked him. Or perhaps, the other brunette with long, dark jet-black hair who had been their second daughter's best friend for a while? All these lovely girls had come from high-standing backgrounds, well-to-do families, and lived in reputable areas on the island.

Yet, although this Marie seemed like a good person, with a kind smile and a good heart, what did she have to offer their Man? It's true she had spent all her teenage years and early twenties doing voluntary work with children and young people locally and abroad and had been attending and running prayer groups for years, but the long and short of it was that her parents did not come from a professional background. They had wanted to believe that social standing did not matter to them; that they would accept whoever their son chose because they loved him and since he was happy with his choice, so they would be too. In their heart of hearts, they always blamed her social standing or lack of it for the irreconcilable differences that separated them and it confirmed to them what they had believed all along. The Man was too good for her.

Wholeheartedly, of course, Amy disagreed. They didn't know the mettle her daughter was made of. And a bit like the traditional Godfather scenario, although Amy would put her own daughter down and criticise her, she wouldn't have anybody else, especially his family, put her down and think any less of her loving, caring, compassionate Marie. She would fight with her life to prove that actually, it was the other way around. The Man hadn't been worthy of her daughter's love. And would never be. But, she had no life to fight with now. Not on the right side of picket line!

Chapter 10

Amy looked on awestruck as the rings were being exchanged and the vows unequivocally proclaimed. That was it. The deed was done. She couldn't cry over milk spilt or not as she had no eyes to shed tears. So what would happen to this sudden sadness, a bit like a grief that was taking hold of her? Where does it now originate? Abide? Where does it go this grief when it subsides? She had no idea, but it did feel like a feeling she remembered from her earlier existence of having had a knot in her tummy and as if her heart were being squeezed leaving her unable to breathe.

She couldn't bear to watch the joy on her Marie's face. She had a feeling that it wouldn't last for long. In her heart of hearts, she hoped she were wrong, but her gut feeling or mother's intuition remained as steadfast now as it had been years earlier—The Man wasn't for Marie and his pious act to win her daughter's heart over wouldn't last long. He would sooner or later expose himself for who he truly was. It would leave Marie devastated. It would change Marie, although she didn't know how at this stage. His heart of steel would not melt but would harden over the years with pride and arrogance, leaving Marie feeling cold, scared, and totally and completely alone in the world. They say that there isn't a loneliness worse than that when one is in a marriage or any relationship for that matter—and Amy was scared that that would be her Marie's lot in years to come. In the meantime, all she could do was watch as everybody ate, drank, and was merry at the sumptuous, yet modest wedding reception.

She was proud of Mike. According to Amy, he had done the right thing and paid for all the food and drink. He wasn't well off but had a heart of gold and wanted to give his only daughter a good send-off. The Man's family looked happy enough, but they hadn't actually done anything to help either financially or otherwise. It had all been down to Marie. The Man would collaborate, but it had all been even at that stage on his own terms. He was still at the stage where he wanted to make a good impression just in case she had had a last minute change of heart, which she had had.

Now Amy recollected how she had watched Marie telling him that she couldn't marry him a couple of months just before the actual wedding. She had listened intently to that conversation. She wasn't going to miss a word and was so proud of how assertive her Marie had been. She had hoped that Marie would see her decision through, as it was the right thing to do—to cancel or postpone the wedding.

Marie had been right all along. He did flirt with other girls all the time. And after his confession of having had a crush on a colleague, she told him in no uncertain terms that the wedding had to be postponed! Hip . . . Hip . . . Hooray! Amy was so glad that nobody could see or hear her. She was in a very privileged position but didn't take advantage of it at this stage. She still just watched carefully and listened intently. It was the first and only moment of happiness since she had been in this state—in this no-man's-land, this limbo. She edged Marie on 'Go, girl. Go, girl, tell him,' she was shouting, or she thought she was anyway. No sound came out, but the words were intended and Marie had somehow been emboldened by her mother's good intentions for her.

However, her moment of rejoicing was very brief and short-lived. She couldn't believe what power The Man had had over her daughter. She couldn't comprehend how her daughter, a strong, intelligent woman who knows her own mind and soul, could be so weak? Was it true love? Was it fear? Manipulation? How would anybody ever know?

How on earth had he convinced her that postponing the wedding for a year was a silly idea and that regardless they should forge ahead? Was her Marie out of her mind? She would regret this. 'Marie,' she shouted, 'you're going to regret this for the rest of your life. Walk away. Now is your chance. You are on the right track. Listen to your mind, heart and gut which are telling you to walk away. If he has a crush on a girl now, before he marries you, what is ever going to stop him from having other crushes on other women? And how can he guarantee that he will not ever act on them? How can you be so naïve, so gullible, so trusting, so believing? Why are you settling for less than the best? Why are you settling for someone who wants you to settle down with and have a family but doesn't love you? Can't love you? Lusts after other women? M-A-R-I-E!' she screamed. Yet, to her utter and sheer disappointment, Marie couldn't hear her and the battle was lost. The Man had won, right there under her nose.

Previously, she had constantly promised Marie that she would be a much better mum on the other side, than on Earth, but she wasn't, was she? She couldn't stop Marie from making the biggest blunder in her life, neither before nor now. She felt more frustrated now than she had been on Earth. However, now, not only did she feel an overwhelming sense of frustration but also, this time, it was accompanied by a sense of responsibility. Had she, Amy, in any way in her lifetime contributed to Marie being in this situation? Aha! This point had never occurred to her before. Before, when overcome by frustration, anger, and guilt, she would just sleep—end of story. Now, she couldn't. Faced with this question, she couldn't rest. She had to look closer as this question wasn't going to go anywhere in a hurry.

The thing was that it was hard looking at this stage. At this stage, it was hurtful to look. This looking was accompanied by a sense of self-criticism and anger at herself for having failed Marie as a mum in so many ways. This was not objective, dispassionate looking. This was very subjective looking coupled with a growing sense of the part she had played in her daughter's lack of self-love, self-esteem, and self-belief. Amy had unintentionally contributed to that. She began to see it as if for the first time. For the first time, she began to hear her own words spoken to Marie with disdain, anger, and hate sometimes, words like, 'selfish . . . you are so selfish . . . you can think of no one but yourself, you can't love anyone, but yourself . . . don't ever say that you are my daughter.' Every time, Marie tried to stand up for herself and not give in to Amy's incessant demands for time, attention, and affection.

Did that have a name? It was beginning to dawn on Amy now that that it might have had a name, but she conveniently couldn't remember it. And, anyhow it wasn't important as the band had started to play and The Man and her Marie opened the dancing on the dance floor.

Oh my goodness, Amy smiled. She did look stunning. Her makeup had been professionally made and so was her longish, brown, curly hair. She had help getting into her wedding dress earlier that morning from a kind neighbour and friend, and she did look beautiful. If only he knew how lucky he was. He would never appreciate her inner and outer beauty. And mind you, neither had she to be honest. She remembered how she had actually envied Marie for her beauty—both inner and outer as she believed they were deeper and much more genuine than hers. She wasn't as good a person as she had thought she had been in the last twenty years, was she? Suddenly, her spirit gave a loud anguished cry and shouted, 'My Lord, my Lord, why have You forsaken me?' 'Where is He?' she thought. 'Please come and save me from myself, please!' She couldn't bear herself any longer, and her torment suddenly resembled that of a woman demented who would pull her own hair, and gnash her teeth and wail and scream, waiting for a redemption that wouldn't come!

If the music stopped, she might be able to doze off, even if it is for a couple of minutes—some respite was all she needed. But the band played on and her spirit hovered in a state of anguish and pain feeling completely powerless to do anything, to change anything, and to have power over anything. She had forfeited that power six months before. Now, she could only watch and wait and feel disgusted at how she had treated this beautiful, innocent, loving creature with so much anger, jealousy, and hate. The thought that Marie might never forgive her weighed heavily on her heart, as she suddenly realised that it would be Marie's forgiveness that would have to set her free. Marie, her Marie, held the key to Amy's future happiness or lack of it. But for how much longer must she suffer for her sins? How long will it take for Marie to forgive her, to set her free? What if Marie did not want to forgive her and never will? What would happen then? If Amy herself managed to stop judging herself, criticizing herself, hating herself, and had the audacity to forgive herself, would that set her free? Or would she still have to wait for Marie to do the same for her? These were questions the catechism book, she remembered reading on the loo again, hadn't answered!

That night was the first night she wished she hadn't done what she had done. That night for the first time came the realisation that her sins weren't the masses she'd missed on Sundays. Her sins hadn't been for not fasting on Good Friday. Her sins weren't having had an affair with her husband's best friend for two years—her sins were of a different nature. Her sins were plenty, and she had chosen not to see them earlier included the beliefs she held about herself and others, the anger, the lack of self-love, the lack of forgiveness, the constant self-criticism, self-judging, the hate towards herself and everyone else, the inability to let go of any of this, and forfeiting of any kind of responsibility for any of this. It was all those things that she had endorsed which had stopped her from being whole—the Amy her God had intended her to be—and had stopped everyone else from being whole, too. All the self-cherishing she had embraced, all the self-centredness she had clung to, unwilling to see beyond her own pain, the pain she had continually caused others and mostly the ones she proclaimed to have loved the most and who most certainly were the ones who had loved her the most—and on the very top of this list was her Marie.

Eventually, the guests tired from dancing the whole night through dispersed and went home. The music stopped, and the newly-weds were chauffeured to their new home. They would consummate their marriage, but it wouldn't change the crush The Man still had on his colleague and friend, and it wouldn't stop Marie's gut telling her that this ceremony wasn't going to change him in any way. He would still need his ego fed by being lusted after by so many other women. Perhaps, to begin with, he would hold out and not act on his lust, but how long that would last for only time could tell.

It was a shame that Marie knew what Amy knew deep down in her heart. So why hadn't she listened to her gut, heart and mind who hadn't stopped warning her about this precarious situation? He had told Marie in no uncertain terms before they got married that if he hadn't settled down with her, he wouldn't find another girl to settle down with and that he would flit from one woman from one woman to another forever.

It begs the question as to whether he did love Marie at all, or if he were just after a good wife and mother to settle down with—a woman of substance, depth, and integrity who would be the backbone of a spineless creature who would depend on her so much. But he would never admit it, and he would never show it and would never allow anyone near enough to see. Once he had warned Marie, as if by warning her before they got married of his need for validation from other women, he would be absolved from all sins, past, present, and future.

He would not let anyone see how much he depended on her steadfastness, faithfulness, and faith. Nobody must know. And for many years to come, Marie did not know either as for many years, he had made her believe that she was the weak one in need of him in her life. He had made her believe that without him, she would be nothing, have no one, have nothing, and go nowhere. He knew too well that this wasn't true. He knew in fact, that it was the other way around, but it was his secret weapon to keep the free spirit of Marie bound to him in spite of his misdemeanours. Perpetuating his position of power, by feeding her words, attitudes, and actions which would leave her doubting herself, her sound judgement, and her very own sanity, he would keep her bound to him. He would make her think that he was right all the time and that any mistrust she had shown over his conduct or misconduct would be just a figment of her wild, jealous imagination. He would make her think that she was losing it just like her mother had! And he would eventually make sure she did. He would invalidate any of her feelings of mistrust and dismiss any claims of infidelity in the face of many significant signs over the years that Marie had picked upon and all in all continue to feed his ego and continue to rule and thrive while she diminished and was nearly demolished.

Yet, would his rule last forever? Would he have her locked up in an institution claiming she were delusional whilst he entertained other women in many interesting and exciting ways? How accurately had he estimated the inner strength, faith, and fortitude of his prized possession?

He had firmly believed that having been a good Catholic girl who had taught catechism until she was twenty or until just a few months before they met, she would be there forever, for him to use and abuse. She would take his mood swings, his sulking, and his words tinged with anger and resentment and she would continually continue to forgive him and come back for more. She would continue to put up with his moods and his sulks that in the end merged into months of him withdrawing into himself and would still always be there. She wouldn't do anything to jeopardise their two boys, either, would she? Amy agreed with him on this one and a sense of quiet desperation took hold of her on her daughter's behalf. But, all she could do was watch and wait.

He knew she had suffered a lot in life and in a way had envied her. Her suffering had made her more open, more loving, and more accepting of the human condition, of her weaknesses, and of the weaknesses of those she loved. His suffering, on the other hand, had made him selfish, sulking, and self-centred. He had hoped that she would have suffered enough for both of them in life and that he would reap the benefits of her goodness and the merits of her good deeds whilst continuing to live a life of selfishness and self-cherishing.

Marie had built herself up spiritually, and the years people had mocked her for dedicating her life to God had borne fruit. She had an unshakable faith and trust in the Lord her God. Not a faith like her mother—her mother's religiosity had led her to despair—no, Marie's faith and spirituality would lead to life and liberation. It would give her the strength and the courage needed to put up with abuse in many shapes and forms, but would it give her the ultimate strength and courage she would need in the future to walk away? To assert her own independence and bring herself to wholeness?

Nobody, at this point in time could guess what would happen twenty years down the line, neither Marie nor Amy and neither could The Man. Now, a happy picture of domestic bliss is what caught an outsider's eye apart from Amy's eye who could see beyond the happy façade right into the two newly-weds' heart of hearts where lust, fear, and infidelity resided.

Chapter 11

It's very hard going having knowledge and insight you cannot act upon or use to your own advantage or to the advantage of anyone else, for that matter. People with integrity know many things about many things and about many people but choose not to use them to their own advantage or to undermine the other person. A hard choice, of course, as sometimes the temptation is great, and although the spirit is willing, the body and mind might be weak. In this state of being, this wasn't the case for Amy. In this state of being, Amy had no choice. She knew what she knew and couldn't use it to her advantage, or to anyone else's. In this case, Amy would have to just watch and wait and see.

Time was ticking, not that she had a clock. No, once again turning to her beloved Marie for a hint of how much time she had been there—in this state of limbo or unknowing—for was all she could do. It was a shame that she couldn't be there as Marie had given birth to a gorgeous little boy who she named Mark. Mark was a good name—one of the people who wrote one of the Gospels was called Mark, she recalled. A good name for the most amazing new born she had ever beheld. She couldn't believe Marie would ever have children as she hadn't been the motherly type although she had worked with children all her life. In fact, that was it. Hadn't working with children of all ages all her life actually put her off having her own? Anyway, it hadn't and for this she was grateful.

She would watch engrossed as this little bundle of joy achieved his first milestones as he would smile for the first time, utter his first word, take his first steps, and continue to grow into an amazing being. These were happy times for Marie, and The Man seemed happy enough too. It kept Amy amused, but gutted that she couldn't be there in person to share in these happy moments. This little man, Mark, would never see her and never know her. 'Well, that could be a blessing,' she thought to herself, 'as hadn't I ruined all the lives of the people I loved and who loved me. At least, from here I cannot ruin anyone's life. I can just watch and feel unbearable remorse!' Unbearable remorse of how utterly selfish she had been and how her happiness, self-preservation, and well-being always came before and sometimes at the expense of everyone else's.

The Man had yearned for a daughter but had a son. His first-born son. He had loved this son in his early years more than he could have ever imagined, and in a way, he had never been able to love anyone else before. Mark opened The Man's heart to love and touched something deep within The Man which softened him for a while. The Man would look at his son and feel so proud of the fruit of his loins. He couldn't believe that something so perfect and so angelic could come out of such an ordinary-looking Man. The Man hadn't been anything special to look at, but he had a charm that appealed to women. A quiet charm. Introverted, dark, and mysterious, he made you want to delve into the deep mysteries of what lay within. Living in his head, nobody was ever allowed in the deepest recesses of his soul, bar Marie who a few times over the years had caught a glimpse of a latent goodness which really wanted to come to fruition.

Marie had longed to be the one who would enable The Man's heart to soften, open, and be able to love and be loved. She had hoped that she would be able to activate that latent goodness and help him multiply it for his own happiness and that of others—for his own well-being and that of others. Alas, in her mother tongue, there is a saying that says that those who live in hope die condemned! A bit of a pessimistic take on life, of course—but, very true in Marie's case. Very true. It was a hope that would destroy her faith in the possibility of people ever changing themselves. Her mother hadn't changed and neither had The Man—both obstinate and proud believing that they were so perfect that there had been nothing that needed looking at or changing. Neither of them would ever take responsibility for hurting others by words, by commission of hurtful acts, or by omission of kind and good ones. No matter how much Marie cared, loved unconditionally or accepted them as they were it didn't change them one little bit. It was years later that Marie realised it wasn't meant to. Nothing would change anyone else, but it would change you and make you a more loving, compassionate and accepting person.

Amy too had hoped that the love that her Marie had lavished on The Man would one day enable his heart to open; she glimpsed at times a dismantling of the great wall that protected his heart, but it would just be a glimpse and the wall would come up as easily as it went down. It was unbearable to watch as she was completely and utterly powerless to do anything about it. It drove her to distraction. At times, in this state, she felt as if she were going insane. Or maybe she was. How do you just watch your own child suffer and do nothing? When a mere mortal, it was fine. She was oblivious of all the suffering that Marie had endured, suffering procured by her, by her 'late' husband, actually it was her who was the late one (and her Maker who still hadn't made an appearance—by Jove He was taking his time, wasn't He?), and by The Man. Ignorance had been bliss on the other side, indeed. Ignorance of Marie's pain and the part she played in making Marie suffer. She would never let Marie forget that it was because of her that she had left the land Down Under to go to that stuffy, dusty island in the middle of the Mediterranean. Marie had to pay for that in many more ways than one.

It seemed to be Marie's lot in life, trying to enable the innate goodness of others to shine through. Trying to reassure others, affirm them, and imbibe them with love so that they would discover their true inner essence which is love and compassion, Marie had firmly believed. It would take her many years to discover and learn that unless the other person cooperated and wanted for it for themselves, the freedom, the love, the happiness that she had wanted for them would all be in vain. Not completely in vain, but it wouldn't go where she had hoped it would and would procure results different to what she would anticipate and hope for.

In Amy's case, she had totally failed, or so she believed. Mainly because Amy did not want for herself what Marie had wanted for her. Whilst Marie had wanted her mother to be fully human, fully alive, happy, whole and at peace with herself, forgiving and loving herself, Amy had wanted to punish herself, to persecute herself, to flagellate herself so that she would never forget her transgressions and never be able to forgive herself her weaknesses. Marie had believed that her mother deserved to be happy, to be forgiven, and to love and be loved, whereas Amy had believed that she deserved punishment. All in all, no matter how hard Marie had tried to help her mother help herself, Amy's lack of cooperation had made it impossible for Marie's efforts and prayers to make any difference to Amy's attitude towards herself, towards life, and towards death.

Would it turn out to be the same with The Man? Would all the love she would lavish on him, all the support she would offer him in his career, following him across to a foreign land so that he could work in the country of his dreams would that bear any fruit? Or would it all be in vain too? Would it make him a nobler, a kinder, a more loving, a more compassionate man? A happier man, fulfilled and at peace with himself and with the world? Whilst Amy believed firmly that this would not be the case, Marie continued to believe that she would melt his heart and be able to turn his heart of stone into a heart of flesh and blood.

Would she hope until the end of time, or would there be a point when she would give up that hope? When hope would turn into despair? When despair would be Marie's best ally—despair would teach Marie a very harsh lesson—a lesson she refused to learn from her experience with her mum and was refusing to learn now. Despair would bring Marie to a point where she would realise that nobody can change anybody else (even if it's for the better so that they may be happier, at peace and be made whole) unless that person had wanted to change. People changed all the time of course, they did. But it was only the people who had wanted to change, that would change. And

Marie would realise this eventually, but would it be too late? Would The Man have such a grip on her by then that this realisation would cut deep within her and lead her, Marie to despair?

Marie had learnt long before this lesson that the only person you could ever change is yourself. And, that the sooner you acknowledged this and believed it, the happier you would be. Amy had tried to tell her this many times over the years. Amy would say, 'Please, Marie don't try to change me it won't work. I know what I have to do to be happy and to get better but I can't do it. I know where all my unhappiness and mental illness comes from but I do not want to move forward. I do not want to do anything that will make me happy.' Marie had had to live with this sense of utter and total powerlessness for her whole life silently watching as her mother entered into self-destructive patterns of behaviour and not being able to do anything about it. She would just have to silently watch and pray and hope that her mother would one day be happy and well. No matter how hard Marie had tried to take a step back and let her mother get on with the business of being dead while living, she couldn't bear to watch her mother destroy herself day by day.

The first time Amy had tried to commit suicide, Marie was about twelve years old. The memory would haunt Marie for the rest of her life. It was the story of Marie's life that she sets out bright and early in the morning hoping for the best at the beginning of a new day when something very bad happens that leaves her paralysed changing something inside of her forever.

She had come home from school on that day anxious to tell her mum all about the class gossip. By now, Marie already knew full well that there were two things and two things only on her mother's mind: leaving her husband and dying. Every day had been a chore since the passionate love affair with Greg or the end of it rather, and picking up the pieces hadn't been easy. In fact, it was Marie who had continually been there to pick up the pieces and support her mother through the mental anguish, guilt, and anger which led to self-destruction.

Anyway, it was getting later and later in the afternoon, and there was no sign of Amy getting up from her siesta. Marie was always alert and vigilant, watching for signs and reading her mother's behaviour. She would have made an amazing psychologist when she grew older. After 5 p.m., Marie was getting really worried. It had been unlike Amy to sleep in later than 5 p.m. It was normally 4.30 p.m. when she drags herself out of the comfort, darkness, and hiding of her bed to continue with going through the motions for the rest of the day. Alas, at 6 p.m., Amy could sustain the apprehension and fear no more. At the risk of being badly told off by Marie for waking her up she tiptoed into the bedroom. Apprehensive and scared she was expecting to be shouted at and that there would be angry words, but she would be relieved as at least her beloved mother, who she had loved more than life itself, was still alive. It was shock and horror when the angry words didn't come or rather nothing came. Amy lay in her bed totally and completely unconscious, and no matter how hard Marie prodded and how loud she begged her mum to wake up no words came no movement came there was a deadly, frightening silence.

Marie panicked. Her heart beating fast, she raced to her neighbour's house who had been her mum's best friend for years, many years earlier and told her what had happened. How her mum would not budge no matter how hard Marie had tried to wake her up she wouldn't. The kind-hearted neighbour Rose, who had loved Marie as if she had been her own daughter, rushed to the house and was accosted by an unconscious Amy ready to die!

Rose ordered Marie to rush to the doctor round the corner and explain what had happened. This was it, Marie had thought. She'd dead! She has died! At that age she still didn't know how it had happened, but she knew she could lose her mother. After what seemed like eons, an ambulance arrived and Amy was ushered to hospital where she was washed out and sent back home the next day. And that was that.

Marie's life was never the same after that. Never. She lived in the constant fear that she would go home one day after school to find that the same thing had happened. Especially, since Amy had explained that there are two options for her: either she would leave the household in which case Marie would have to hold the fort and take care of her dad and brother or she would commit suicide but she would do it right the next time. She would go through with it.

Amy had explained to Marie at that stage that although she had married Mike, she had never loved him. Never. She wanted to get rid of an authoritarian father who had forbade a former boyfriend whom she had madly fallen in love with to go anywhere near her. That was her revenge. She would tell no one. Not even her mother. Her mother, God rest her soul had had to endure many things in life and put up with a demented husband who having been an open gunner in World War II had nightmares and flashbacks for the rest of his life. They were not offered counselling in those days and so the whole family suffered his bouts of physical and verbal violence, and everybody lived in utter and sheer fear of upsetting him.

Had it been an act of defiance, a seventeen-year-old trying to make a point? An act of foolishness thinking that two wrongs would make a right? Whatever it was, Amy declared to Marie for the first time, the first night back from hospital that she had never loved Mike, although he had been madly in love with her and would never love another woman in the same way he had loved her. After that, Amy would tell Marie this story repeatedly, over the years reminding Marie that she did not love Mike and that she never had and never will. But, he mustn't know. She did not tell Marie about her passionate love affair with his best friend Greg, that little, insignificant secret she kept to herself. She did explain to Marie though, that she was a saint with a past and had been a great sinner.

All this lying didn't do Amy any favours. You can pretend sometimes but, not all the time. Sometimes the truth catches up with you and takes you by surprise. What you do then is entirely up to you for some, that moment is the moment they vow to own up to the truth and seek the path to enlightenment. For others they can't face the magnitude of the lies the damage they'd caused the cost of the repair the responsibility they would have to take so they would cave in to despair. The latter is what Amy chose unfortunately. Not at that time. Although she had tried many times over the years. The day she actually did forge ahead and commit the deed was many, many years after the first ever episode.

In the meantime, every time she would try to end it once and for all, it would be Marie who would save her. Sadly, it marred Marie's existence as she lived with a constant fear that her worst nightmare would one day come true as it had—on a day when she and Amy had exchanged words; on a day when she, Marie had to go to work as she had been leading a school outing and thinking she was indispensable, and being responsible ignored Amy's plea for attention; on a day when it was nearly Christmas and Marie's engagement to The Man; on a day when Marie had not expected it to happen and had no inkling that that day would be the day that would change her forever!

About a few years after the first incident, there were a couple more, but there was one particular evening when Amy had had an overdose of pills and alcohol and was hoping that she would not wake up. She had tried to overdose a few times by now with no success, but was adamant that this time she had cracked it.

Marie had heard Amy fumble and puff in the kitchen and had a gut feeling that something was not right. Marie, the ever vigilant one, the responsible one, the one who bore the brunt of all the lies, of all the deceit and of all the sadness. Marie's ears pricked up for more clues. Was her mother at it again? Oh please God, not again! Not another trip to the hospital in the dead of night. Oh please God, not again! She prayed in her head in anguish.

She thought about the situation often, more often than she had liked. The ghost of this happening to her one day was her companion to bed every night for many years. Unlike many girls her age who would go to bed with thoughts of romance and love, Marie would go to bed with fear in her gut and a paralysing sense of powerlessness permeating her whole being. That sense of powerlessness, of sheer and utter powerlessness was unbearable. She wanted to die. Her mother, more than anything else in world had wanted to die. Whilst, most of us struggled to stave off the dread of death, Amy relished it! Relished the thought that her soul would fly to heaven as soon as she would have the courage to end it all. She had it all sussed out. All planned out. He, her God, of course, would come in his floating white robe and long white beard and judge her. He would perhaps judge her harshly and she would have to go to a place she had learnt had been called purgatory. Purgatory would be where she would be purged of all her sin like gold being purified by fire or something like that, anyway and finally reach her heavenly haven to rest in His arms and live happily ever after.

Marie, on the other hand, did wonder that night what to do. She did ponder whether to listen to her gut feeling which was telling her to check on Amy, or to conveniently ignore it and go to sleep as she was in bed already. 'Anyway, why would I want to stop my mum from committing suicide?' she pondered. She wasn't sure she endorsed euthanasia; at that point, she didn't know what she endorsed and what she believed it was all a blur. Even if she thought she had all the answers to everything else in life—the arrogance of youth, maybe?—but, to this question, she sadly had no answer. There was no one to turn to in the dead of night, as each of these episodes seemed to happen at that time 'Why?' she wondered. She believed in her heart of hearts at that time that she had no right to keep saving a woman who did not want to be saved. Who was she, Marie, to decide whether her mum lives or dies? Who was she, Marie, bearing the brunt, all the responsibility for her mother's well-being to say whether it is best for her mum to stay embodied on Earth, when without a shadow of a doubt, the only thing that Amy had wanted to do was to die? What gave Marie the right to play God? What gave Marie the right to stop her mother from achieving her lifelong dream to rest in peace? It was as if by stopping Amy, Marie was asserting that she knew more than Amy herself what would make her happy. And did she?

It pained Marie constantly to live with and take care of a mother whose only wish in life was to die. Marie reacted to this in an unusual way. Marie relished life and loved life as she believed she had a mission to fulfil and that she was put here for a reason. Would one of those reasons be to save Amy from herself and stop her this time? Or would her reason for being there a daughter of Amy be to let her die?

Being only sixteen years old and having to make this decision in the middle of night completely on your own is nothing but terrifying. No fifteen-year-old or any child of any age should be faced with such a dilemma. And yet, Marie realised later on in life that hundreds perhaps even thousands of teenagers faced the same dilemma she had faced that night—and it tore her to pieces to realise that. She would do everything in her power as the years rolled on to alleviate the pain of people in these situations and prayed to God that night that whatever the outcome, if through all this suffering, anguish, and pain, she would be able to help one person, just one person in the future then all of this would not be in vain. It would have been worth it.

She heard footsteps approaching her closed bedroom door, and Amy's voice interrupted her utter loneliness as she asked if she could come in. Marie, of course, was relieved that Amy had come in one piece, sane and conscious for a chat. Phew! No damage done so far. Alas, Amy would then utter the most dreaded words Marie would hear: 'I love you, Marie, you know that, don't you? You know, don't you, that whatever happens, I love you? I want you to know that and to remember that, Marie.'

As those words were being uttered with utter sincerity and humility, Marie's heart stopped. Her gut feeling, she knew was right. And she couldn't do anything to stop Amy from going through with her premeditated act of complete self-destruction.

'Have you just done something stupid, Mum? Have you just been taking pills? Is that what all the sneaking about and rustling in the kitchen was about? Mum, please tell me the truth,' she pleaded.

At this stage, Marie had made her choice. She would have to interfere. She would have to keep her mum alive, otherwise how would she be able to live with herself? Not doing anything to stop her is as good as killing her herself she thought. Not quite, but she would feel totally responsible if she didn't intervene and Amy would die. She struggled, as, on the other hand, she still felt like it wasn't her call, it was Amy's call, and if this is what Amy wanted, then why couldn't she respect her wishes? Was it through selfishness that she had wanted Amy to hang around? She was about to sit her GCEs and this wouldn't have been a good time. But, would there ever be a good time? She still felt like she was playing God and depriving her mother from what she really desired wholeheartedly. It wouldn't go down well with Amy if she announced she were turning her in and calling an ambulance. Or worse, wake Mike up from his deep sleep and make him take her. That wouldn't go down well with him either. And what about Marie's younger brother, the one with the hazel green eyes, where was he? He'd have to come to the hospital too. What an inconvenience for everyone involved, especially for Amy whose plan would be ruined before she had time to say boo to a goose.

Suddenly, Marie jumped to her feet, woke Mike up, and lo and behold, before everybody knew it, they were at the accident and emergency reliving the same nightmare in the dead of night, they had lived through a few times previously. The pain in Marie's heart cut through like a dagger and her heart bled not blood, but pain, anguish, fear, and even anger, maybe. Anger? At whom? At what? She didn't know maybe at life, at circumstances, at her lot in life and at why had it have to be her to watch and be able to change nothing? Anger at having to mother her mother, anger at not being loved as a daughter ought to be, anger at all the responsibility, at the futility of life and the meaninglessness of all this suffering.

Now the roles were reversed. How amusing. Now, it was Amy's turn to watch, in silence, as her daughter suffered in this unhappy marriage. She wanted happiness for her daughter now even more than her own. How bizarre. She had never had this notion before—not even as a mother, on Earth. Before, she had been so engrossed in her own unhappiness, she had often been jealous of Marie's happiness. Now, she would watch and pray that she could take on her own daughter's suffering, pain, and loneliness onto herself. Now, she would wish wholeheartedly that she could make her daughter's insecurities, uncertainties, and unhappiness go away, but how? A deep sense of frustration and anger began to arise within her spirit. Where the sense of anger was within her spirit, she could not tell, although it seemed more towards the middle of her spirit rather than the bottom or the top, but she couldn't locate its position exactly.

So, now it was her time to suffer with her Marie the same way her Marie had suffered with her. Now, it was her turn to wish Marie's unhappiness away and feel anguish in her heart centre as she realised there was not one thing on Earth or beyond that she could do to make her daughter's suffering go away. If this is how Marie had felt throughout her life on Amy's behalf, then Amy thought Marie had suffered quite a bit with her and carried quite a bit of her burden. Why hadn't she been able to see any of this before? Why was it taking so long for things to dawn on Amy? The realisation of how much her daughter had suffered on her behalf wasn't an easy one. She, Amy, had been so self-absorbed in her own pain, anguish, and suffering that Marie's efforts to alleviate the pain had gone totally unnoticed and completely unappreciated. Is this why Amy was still hanging on in this place? What else would she have to realise before she were allowed to go?

'That was a loud shriek,' thought Amy as it stopped her reverie and gave her a bit of respite. It wasn't exactly a shriek, more like a scream, well lots of screaming actually. She peered on as she perceived Marie's legs open astride on a white bed, screaming her head off, as a tiny head appeared at her cervix. She was giving birth, and this time the little son she bore, they named David.

David, the fruit of his loins and her love, was the most adorable baby Amy had ever seen. To Marie, he had looked like a squashed aubergine as he came out, but after having been wiped down and settled to feed, she too decided that this adorable creature must have been one of the most amazing sights she had ever beheld—after the birth of Mark, of course.

The couple had moved to the land of his dreams, and David being born there represented all of The Man's hopes for the future, his dreams coming true. But, at this stage, The Man had already changed beyond recognition, and his heart was like the walled city of his homeland—strong, imposing yet impenetrable. Marie knew in her heart of hearts that he had changed.

She didn't know why, what, and wherefore, but nonetheless, she knew and it caused her great insecurity, uncertainty, and pain.

Marie had changed too. 'Motherhood,' she thought. She began to give much more attention to their growing eldest son. The Man grew restless and very jealous of the relationship Marie and Mark had. Marie would spend what seemed like hours putting him to bed. She would read him a story, then chat to him, sing to him and then chat a bit more and would always take the time to answer his inquisitive mind and very well-thought-out questions. The Man would sit downstairs in front of the tellie waiting for Marie to come downstairs, his voice betraying the resentment he felt at how much love his wife had to offer and how she so generously lavished it onto their eldest son. He didn't believe how much she had loved him. He didn't want to believe. It suited him not to believe. That way, he could justify his misdemeanours and misconduct and rationally and callously blame it all onto her.

Amy was getting more and more frustrated. It was her turn now to watch and wait in a state of utter and complete powerlessness. She began to relate, for the first time ever, how it must have felt for Marie all those years earlier. It began to dawn on her, how much her Marie had actually loved her—really loved her and how she had wanted her happiness more than Amy herself had done. There was nothing she could do now. Amy watched in complete silence as the gulf between Marie and The Man continued to grow. Amy continued to watch as The Man turned to other women for affirmation, reassurance, intimacy, and pleasure. She watched and yearned to be able to warn her Marie and reassure her that her gut was right and that her suppositions were not unfounded, but she couldn't. She could only watch and wait, and wait and watch.

Chapter 12

Marie couldn't believe what she saw as she peered into the mirror. She wasn't happy with the mirror that morning and looked even more closely. Her eyes must have deceived her. No, maybe it was the light. You could never tell in this God-forsaken country, Marie thought what you saw in the mirror. One day you looked fine. Then a month later, the sun would come out and all the blemishes and facial hair would begin to show. 'It's not that it hadn't been there previously, of course, but ignorance can be bliss, and what you can't see, can't hurt you,' Marie mused. But, this particular morning, she could see as she detected a white hair! Wasn't she too young for white hairs? She realised that they are called grey in this country, probably to match the constant grey sky, the grey moods she had been sinking quite deeply into lately, the thick grey clouds that had a habit of gathering together causing havoc to her world, obscuring her dearly beloved sunshine.

The appearance of grey hairs is no big deal for most people these days. A bottle of hair dye bought cheaply at the chemist or supermarket can make it go away and one can easily pretend that that never was or had been. So why is it such a big deal for Marie that morning? It wasn't that she was barely over thirty and nowhere near prepared for the onset of ageing. It wasn't that she was scared that The Man would mind—he had been grey since eighteen anyway. It wasn't that she would have to dye her hair for decades to come. So what was it?

She was convinced that morning that she was jinxed! Jinxed! The evil eye and the lot was something quite hot in her homeland and widely accepted. People would wear a cross to keep the evil eye at bay, or an eye on a gold or silver chain. Good luck eyes were stuck on traditional fishing boats and put on the old colourful traditional buses on which Marie had travelled on all her teenage years to protect the owner of such a good luck eye from the much-dreaded and much-endorsed evil eye. Marie had never actually been into these things herself although she had been very aware of how people of all walks of life went about life believing in such shall we say, tales? But, today, to poor Marie, first thing in the morning, this didn't appear as a tale at all.

She had cracked it. She knew it! It had to be Amy. Amy had jinxed her! From wherever Amy had been, Marie was convinced that morning that Amy had jinxed her. 'And why on earth would she think that? Why?' Amy wondered.

Of course, Amy had to go back. She had to force herself to go back to the days when her spirit roamed the Earth in a physical body. Amy hadn't been a fitness freak like Marie—it hadn't been in their culture at that time, and anyway she had been too dosed up on Anafranil and lithium to be able to walk at times let alone keep herself fit and trim. But, she did her best at all times to look her best. She would buy nice clothes for Sunday mass and to go out in on Saturday nights to the promenade or to the capital to play bingo. She would have her hair cut every six weeks without fail. And although she wasn't a make-up person, she would occasionally wear some red lipstick and nail varnish which would really suit her. She had looked stunning in the photos of her youngest son's First Holy Communion in her pink pleated dress (as was the fashion in those days), a delicate pink feather in her hair, and beautiful brown lipstick to accentuate her beautiful brown tan.

There was one thing she hadn't been into, of course and, that was hair dye. She would not have her hair dyed! And to be honest, until that fatal day six years earlier at the ripe age of forty-three when she had decided to end it all, she had hardly had any grey hair, apart from a few sparse ones occasionally showing their head. She hadn't realised how lucky she had been. She was one of those fortunate women who did not have to worry about going grey in their thirties and spend a fortune and a lot of time dying their hair.

She did have an issue though with the couple of white hairs that did sprout up every now and then. She wouldn't be able to see them properly, and because of very poor hand—eye coordination, she wouldn't be able to pluck them effectively either. Now, as for plucking grey hairs, we are told time and time again that it mustn't be done! 'For every grey hair you pluck, you get seven growing in its place' is the old wives' tale! Or perhaps, not? Anyway, to cut a long story short, there was a way around of all this phaffing about and it was simple. Amy would have a pair of tweezers ready in her hand, and as soon as Marie would make an appearance in the house, the request would be made: 'Marie, can you pluck my grey hairs today? I haven't got many.' An argument would ensue. Marie would maintain that seven would grow for each one she would pluck. Amy would maintain she absolutely did not care. She just wanted them out.

It wasn't really the fact that Marie really believed seven would grow for each one she would pluck; it was more a matter of principle. Whereas, Amy believed that she was hanging onto life to spare her Marie the grief of having to take care of her brother and father Marie believed she had been doing that for years anyway. Whereas, Amy believed that she loved Marie so much she wouldn't end it all before Marie would finish Uni., Marie believed that her mum would never let her forget each day how much she had wanted to die but lived on for Marie's sake.

All that Marie had to do was to pander to her mum's every wish in return; otherwise, Amy would send Marie on a massive guilt trip, and most times, it just wasn't worth it. Either that or she would disown her, reject her, and tell her how selfish and self-centred she was and how she was unable to think of anyone but herself.

Amy recalled once again how Marie had spent her teenage years as a member of the local catechism centre teaching children from four to eleven years. She would also teach people older than her later on in the evening. It wasn't an easy life. Whereas, all of Marie's peers were going to the cinema and out drinking and dancing, Marie would be teaching seven days a week from 5 p.m. to 9 p.m. on Monday to Saturday and most of the day on Sunday. It was a massive commitment—a commitment that Marie took very seriously. How she actually got into this at the age of fourteen is a story for another day, but Amy detested this centre with her whole heart and took every opportunity to dig at Marie trying to get her to stop going. Then maybe she would have her daughter back. Then maybe her daughter would be able to walk the dog with her a bit more often than she had done. Then maybe her daughter would just stay at home and be with her.

It was no secret that Amy detested the fact that Marie attended this centre as Amy did not hide it. It was a shame as ironically the fact that Marie had been going to this centre meant that Marie could support Amy in the way she had needed it the most. And how was that?

Over the years, Amy's guilt had taken on enormous proportions and her past instead of resting in peace in the distance became more and more real much more real than the present. The obsession with the past would not let Amy rest. It was as if Amy was held captive by this monster eating at her, a monster depriving her of sleep, peace, and mental health—the monster of guilt and the obsession with the past.

She could not stop thinking of Greg, and she would not. She would not let go and often had said this to Marie in no uncertain terms. She knew what made her mentally ill. She knew that this obsession with the past and the what could have been(s) coupled with the guilt were destroying her. But what was the other option? To be whole, fully human, fully alive? Did she deserve that? Did she actually want it or was she too scared to be happy and whole again?

So, she would turn to Marie in her hour of need not once, not twice but sometimes more than three times a day asking Marie about the nature of her thoughts whether they were a sin? Were they a sin if they just appeared out of nowhere and she didn't want them? What if they appeared out of nowhere, she didn't want them but would enjoy them, would that constitute a sin? And the questions went on and on and on.

It continued to make Marie feel very responsible not so much for her mother's physical well-being now that Mike hadn't hit her for years and the threat of going home and finding her mother murdered had subsided, but more for her mother's mental, psychological, and spiritual well-being. She would reiterate to her mum that whatever the scenario, it wasn't a sin that a thought is a thought and especially if you didn't want it, then it wasn't a sin! It took a lot out of Marie this constant demand to reassure Amy, but she did it wholeheartedly, nonetheless. She worried about the well-being of her mum the whole time knowing that her mum lived in constant mental torment and rarely was her mind allowed to rest.

It was a good job that Marie did attend the centre, however. She had had an avid spiritual life and found that which is in everything and within which everything exists; she found love and acceptance. But, above all, she found an angel in the form of a spiritual master who loved Marie, believed in her, and listened to her. Like a surrogate dad, he supported her and would always listen to her stories of misery and hardship at home. How, after all the times Marie would reassure Amy, Amy would then turn on her and call her names like selfish, egoistic, not able to love anyone but herself, self-centred, uncaring, unloving and any other insult she could think of. These words used to hurt Marie to no end as they were very untrue, unfair and meant to hurt. It was Amy's way of retaliating every time she did not get her way. Marie believed that no matter how many names she was called by both Mike and Amy, no matter how rejected she felt, lonely, scared, and alone in a violent and unpredictable home, her God loved her beyond words, accepted her as nobody else did or would, and would take care and protect her like her parents never could. So inside, Marie grew stronger and stronger, as her faith in the love her God had for her became evident in her everyday life.

But when Amy would then appear with tweezers in one hand and mirror in the other asking Marie to pluck her white hairs, it was no wonder Marie would refuse. Hadn't she done so much for her mother all her life? Didn't she worry about the well-being of her mother the way a mother would worry about her daughter or son? Didn't she try to do her best to keep her company at all times to the best of her ability? Wasn't she always trying to lighten her burden, listening wholeheartedly and reassuring constantly? Surely, plucking her white hairs was beyond the call of duty, and although she obliged a couple of times through the fear of being rejected, she put her foot down in the end and flatly refused to have anything to do with plucking of white hair or any hair for that matter.

After these six years, had Amy actually forgiven Marie for having spent her youth at the centre? Had she now, after six years of watching, forgiven Marie for having gone to Sicily and leaving her for one whole month two consecutive summers? That hadn't bothered Amy so much as the trip to India. What was it about the trip to India that had bothered Amy so much? For the two consecutive summers in Sicily she had forgiven Marie. Amy had began to realise by now that she was meant to have taken more responsibility for her own well-being and should not have depended totally on drugs and on Marie for emotional and psychological support.

For dedicating her youth to God by teaching at the centre and not being there for her in the way she had wanted her to be, she had forgiven her also. In fact, it hadn't been a case of forgiving Marie as much as the realisation of how selfish and self-centred and demanding and unreasonable and manipulative Amy had been. This realisation of how she had behaved towards Marie all those years had come to Amy as a massive shock.

And it wasn't so much a question of having forgiven Marie so much as to whether Marie had forgiven her. Marie looked into the mirror today, six years after her mother's death, angry at the appearance of her grey hair. 'Why did she have to jinx me? Why couldn't she leave me alone now? Does she have to punish me even now for the things she had always wanted me to do which I didn't? Is this punishment for refusing to pluck her grey hairs all those years before?' Marie felt like screaming to the mirror to on the wall. Life wasn't fair, Marie concluded! And no, she hadn't forgiven Amy for her unreasonable demands. No, she hadn't forgiven Amy for not taking responsibility for her own well-being and inability to let go of the past and to forgive herself for her past transgressions. And no, she hadn't forgiven Amy for having been so insensitive to her needs. And no, she hadn't forgiven Amy for always thinking of herself, her needs, her discomfort, her pain regardless of how it made others feel. And no she hadn't forgiven Amy for allowing her guilt to eat away at her and inwardly destroy her. And no, she hadn't forgiven Amy for ending it all on the day when she and her had had a row! That had been below the belt and had left Marie bereft beyond words can describe. That Marie didn't know if she could ever forgive her, actually.

In the meantime, Marie still had to grapple with an emptiness inside like she had never known before. Not, a spacious, beautiful emptiness full of love and light and a luminosity. No. An emptiness like that of a narrow, dark, humid, stinking, bottomless pit from which she could not emerge. And now, to make matters worse, she had to grapple with grey hairs on top of all that! 'What a life!' she mused.

Chapter 13

It would be seven years from that fatal day when Marie had left the house in a huff not taking Amy's request to be taken to the mental hospital too seriously. Imploring and pleading with her mother to let it rest and asking her to hang on in there as it would be Marie's engagement in a couple of days and Christmas day the day after that. This day neither Amy nor had Marie ever forgotten. Marie thought about it today.

The seventh anniversary since her beloved mum had passed away, or jumped into oblivion. It had seemed like seven years of famine where she was starving inside and longed to be nourished by a joy, a peace, and a harmony she only had a faint memory of as they had deserted her seven years earlier on her mother's demise. As for Amy, it had been seven long years of waiting that she couldn't forget and couldn't believe. Seven years, and He still hadn't made an appearance. What a liberty! What a f**king liberty as one of Marie's favourite British comedians would say. Leaving her there to wait for seven years?! If she had known it was going to be this bad, she would have hung on to her body for much, much longer but how could she have known that this was what awaited her? Seven years of doing nothing, of watching and waiting and waiting and watching was a very long time indeed.

Had she really done it on that particular day to spite Marie? Had that been the impetus she had needed to give her the drive, the motivation to do it? These questions tortured her and where they came from she had no idea.

What she was sure about was that these questions were not going anywhere and hadn't for the last seven years. These questions were going to cling to her for dear life and were not going to dissolve, were not going to cease until she accepted the responsibility for her actions and realised the damage her selfishness had caused. These were questions that wanted to and needed to be looked at rather than answered.

She wanted to run, to escape, to jump from the bastions again, perhaps? Now that wasn't an option in this state of being! Sleep, maybe? She hadn't had a proper night's sleep for seven years. That's enough to drive anybody mad. She needed respite from this sense of torment and torture and sense of utter and total shame that would cling to her as her skin would have clung to the rest of her body. She remembered that whenever questions such as these arose before, she would be reassured by Marie that it was all OK, that there was nothing to worry about, that she could forfeit any responsibility, and that Marie would shoulder that responsibility on her behalf.

But now here, there was no Marie to bail her out. Now, here she had to face these questions whether she wanted to or not, whether she felt brave enough or not, whether she was in the mood or not. Here there was nowhere to run. She would have to take full responsibility for her actions, all of them, and questioning her motivation would be a helpful tool to ascertain how much awareness she had actually had of hurting others. Being mentally ill, when embodied, had been so convenient. It absolved you from all responsibility. But, here there was nobody to absolve her and no label would absolve her and her selfishness and self-centredness.

Here she would have to see what she had done, admit it, and take responsibility for it and then after that, with eyes wide open, she would have to absolve herself. Absolve herself! She had never been able to do that before. She hadn't forgiven herself all her life, how could she forgive herself now? How would she be able to forgive herself, after having recognised the full magnitude of the damage her selfishness and self-absorption had caused?

And would Marie ever forgive her? Ah, how apt to be thinking about absolving herself and about forgiveness just as Marie was pulling up in the car park of the Catholic Abbey! How strange! What was Marie doing here? Wasn't she working today? Who was she here to see and why? Amy prayed as she followed Marie into the abbey. She did pray for forgiveness of her sins by God, the God she had so devoutly prayed to every single minute of every single day of her life.

She still couldn't get herself to forgive herself, to let go, and to choose life over death, well-being over illness, happiness over sadness, and joy over sorrow. Sad. It meant that she would have to wait a while longer until she came to her Promised Land. She still made excuses for her behaviour and still couldn't shoulder responsibility for what damage she had procured. She did pray for Marie too! She prayed that Marie would forgive her. But, today, it wasn't Amy who Marie needed to forgive. Today, Marie wasn't at the abbey praying to forgive Amy although Marie knew she had to come to that point and sometimes had glimpses of having forgiven her mother. Today, Marie was desperate to begin to forgive herself and let go as her own guilt was driving her insane and eating her up inside, tearing her to pieces day after day, leaving her weary, tired, and very sad.

Marie couldn't live like this anymore. She felt as if she were going mad. 'Seven years of drought,' she thought—seven years of not feeling the peace, the contentment when she lay in bed, of a pure and loving heart. It was no use that all her loved ones reiterated it hadn't been her fault; she couldn't have known; she couldn't have guessed, there was a bigger picture of which Marie had been unaware of. That all passed her by.

It was no use that her loved ones, trying to reassure her, would say that Amy would have done it anyway, if not on that day then on another day soon after. The Man himself had been very good at this to begin with, but then stopped partly thinking that Marie had had it all sorted out. Marie came here to ask for forgiveness, to be healed, to be able to move on, to forgive herself and to forgive Amy for wanting to make her feel guilty for the rest of her life, or so she thought. Manipulating someone while alive is one thing Marie could cope with to a degree. She had got used to the mental, emotional, and psychological abuse as she didn't know any better, as it were. But to continue to manipulate someone seven years after you have left your embodied existence is cruel, very cruel indeed. It leaves the other person feeling like they are fighting against a ghost, punching a fist through thin air! Marie still did not have a clue where Amy ended and she started. She did not know who she was, what she believed about life that wasn't a reaction to or against what Amy had believed.

Father Nicholas was a very good and holy monk, a very holy soul, indeed. It didn't take him long to proclaim to Marie that her mum had had a hold on her for the last seven years after her demise as much as she had had on her in her lifetime if not more. A psychic link, he had called it. It needs to be severed. And the sooner it can be severed, the better the quicker you will be set free! He had said to Marie. And who could tell that it would take another seven years for that psychic link to be severed. What had Marie actually ever done in life but try to make her mum better and try to take care of her emotional and psychological needs, and what does she get in return? She was surprised that she didn't turn out bitter and twisted, untrusting and very angry at life's unseeming merciless consequence for an action for which she herself hadn't been directly responsible. 'Life wasn't fair,' she thought once again. But she got on with it. She had a husband, two boys, a part-time job, a house to run, chores and errands to attend to so there was no time to stop and wallow in self-pity or to stop and make a fuss. Therefore, on the outside, she continued to get on with things, and it was business as usual.

On the inside, it was a different story, a different story indeed. There was a terrible longing to forgive and be forgiven. To forgive herself and to forgive Amy. Amy, on the other hand, also waited and waited to forgive herself and to forgive Marie for not taking her too seriously on that fateful morning. The two women waiting. One on Earth doing everything in her power to let go and set herself free of a guilt haunting her soul, the other on the other side, how can she do it?

Marie would get Father Nicholas on her case, and this holy man would help sort herself out. Who would Amy be able to enrol on this mission?

The sad and scary answer to that was nobody. The awful thing about Amy's situation was in her case, in her state of being it all had to be worked out by her, on her own. She would have to reach her own conclusions as to what she should have learnt in life, become aware of the consequences of her actions and the suffering she had caused, and feel remorse for those actions and for forfeiting responsibility for those actions; she would then have to resolve not to do it again if she were in a similar situation, and finally, she would have to forgive herself. All of this Amy would now have to procure on her own. No wonder it had taken her seven years and she hadn't made much progress. There was nobody to urge her on, apart from Marie. Every so often, what Marie thought, did, or said would remind Amy of something important she would have to face, an abominable action she would have committed. At that point, Amy would have to sit with that pain and wait until it subsided. She would just have to grin and bear it and this she had been doing for the last seven years. But the incidents she had been being reminded of were numerous, and if it had taken so long, how long would it take before she dealt with the whole lot? An eternity?

Marie began to bare her soul to this holy priest who thought it necessary Marie confide in him from her earliest memories. He believed that once these memories were 'healed', they would not hold any more power over Marie and the process would set her free. Amy watched and listened in suspense as her 'sins' were being unveiled, uncovered. Oh my God! Marie wasn't going to actually tell Father Nicholas what Amy had done to her, Freddie the Teddy was she? Not that. What had she been still carrying that for? And anyway, hadn't Amy taught Marie that these things were not to be divulged to strangers and people to whom this was not their business? It was as if Amy's eyes began to widen (figuratively speaking) and to water as Marie recounted the incident of when Freddie the Teddy was shred to smithereens on the pavement by a big, sharp knife held by Amy in front of all of Marie's neighbours and friends.

Marie recounted how that precious teddy, one of the few remaining artefacts from her homeland Down Under, was dissected and all the foam filled the pavement and the gutter whilst Marie wailed and begged Amy to stop. 'Stop! Stop! Please! I'll be good! I'll share him with Susie, but please stop!' And the neighbour, Susie's mum and Amy's best friend, also had pleaded with Amy to stop. But Amy was too angry at Marie for not sharing her teddy with Susie who could sometimes be a pain in the butt and was quite annoying to Marie many times and carried on regardless of the wailing and pleas to stop. It was an incident which marred Marie for life unbeknown to Amy. It seemed that other people were able to make mistakes in life, and things would turn out OK in the end. They would make mistakes but other people and life would be forgiving. This incident began to teach Marie that when she made a mistake, it wasn't OK; it wasn't going to be made OK by anyone and nobody was going to forgive her and life would hold it against her as long as she lived. It taught her that the punishment most of the time doesn't fit the crime or that the punishment is always much greater, much harsher than the crime itself. It made Marie judge herself very harshly in adult life and it made it hard for Marie to get a fair sense of her mistakes as she would always judge herself much more harshly than any other person who loved her would.

Anyway, it seemed like one of life's little miracles when many years later Susie made it up to Marie. Susie hadn't forgotten the incident either. She had felt guilty herself for having got Marie into so much trouble but they were only children the pair of them and neither of them at that time could have envisaged the damage one tiny, child argument could cause what lasting damage it would leave, what a scar it would sculpt. Susie had offered (unsolicited) a soft, furry purse an uncle had brought her from the land Down Under as a gesture of goodwill as an atonement she had said to Marie to make up for the murdered and mutilated teddy that day.

That was a day of healing for both Marie and Susie, and they hugged and cried as their offspring jumped up and down water slides that hot, sunny afternoon. The girls, over the rest of their adult lives, had become the best of friends like sisters even and through thick and thin and through life's ups and downs of which both had had many they stood by each other. And although the miles divided them as Marie relocated due to The Man's career (and many other reasons, of course!), they remained in touch, but more importantly remained in each other's minds and hearts.

As Amy listened in stunned silence, she began to see and comprehend some of the damage she had caused to this daughter she had actually loved so much and began to sob. She couldn't believe now looking back, how she could have done that. She couldn't believe that having loved her Marie so much she could have humiliated her so badly. She couldn't believe the pain this incident had still caused Marie. She was beginning to see how mean she had been and how much pain and hurt she had caused to someone she thought she had loved so much.

She was there stuck in this state of being, being faced with her cruelty to her then six-year-old daughter and had to stay with the sense of shame at what she had done. She silently prayed that on that day Marie would forgive her. Little did she know that Marie had long since forgiven her, but the aftermath of that memory had stayed with Marie till then. Marie had never wished her mother ill because of this incident. In fact, it had hurt so much only because Marie had loved her mum with all the love the heart of a little six-year-old can muster and longed to be loved by her mum in the same way. And, Amy realised now how short she had fallen of this! Again, remorse hit her hard in the heart area, and it seemed to make her whole ethereal body ache and writhe and contort in a way a human body would when in agony and in severe unbearable pain similar to that of childbirth. She would one day have to help Marie and put things right but when that time would come she did not know. Presently, she could only wish she hadn't acted with so little regard to how her actions could make others feel, so wrapped up had she been in her own narrow view of reality.

There were many other memories Father Nicholas would encourage Marie to uncover. He would help her heal of any remnants of guilt that were preventing Marie from moving on. He would help her confront the nature of her guilt, the uselessness of it, the futility of it and help her come to a place where she would feel safe inside to let it go. At that point, the past would not hold her captive anymore. She would roam the earth bound on the outside by society-imposed rules and regulations, but inside, she would be set free! She would walk with a twinkle in her eye and a song in her heart, but most of all the contentment of a pure conscience she had known before would also return. Why did it seem as though she was constantly punishing herself for things she hadn't done? Punishing herself even, for things that had been done to her by other people?

Amy did not know how long it would take for her to be able to forgive herself. Now that she was faced by the trauma she had caused, it was hard for her to forgive herself. But she knew her God loved her beyond imagining, and if she wished it enough, prayed for it enough, and trusted enough, it would be given her one day—one day when the time was right and she was ready, it would all be made right. One day, the scars would heal. One day, Marie would look at those scars and not remember who put them there or why. She would look at them as if they didn't matter, because they won't. Whether they were scars put there by The Man or by Mike or by Amy, it wouldn't matter as they would not hurt anymore or bleed or water or ache. They would just be visible as a mark, that's all. Marie, of course, longed for this day and so did Amy.

Alas, Marie knew it wouldn't be one fine day. It would take what would seem like eons for this to happen. She sometimes wondered if she would be lucky for all of this to happen while she were still in her human existence, or would she have to wait until she crossed onto the other side, or just before, before total and utter healing would take place and she would be totally set free from her sins and the sins of her ancestors thrust upon her. She would not want those sins to go onto the next generation. She would do anything for this cruelty, this abuse, and this dysfunction to stop with her. She was willing to pay the price. And the price she did pay in the shape and form of an exile to a land of cold climate and cold hearts, an exile away from the love of her father and brother, an exile which would facilitate a new start, a fresh start for her, for the Man and for their children. She was exiled to stop what seemed like monsters from eating up her offspring, fresh into the world. Little did she count on all the other implications of her exile with The Man!

Anyway, it was thanks to Father Nicholas at the end of the day that Marie's heart began to become alive again. The peace, the joy, and the sense of contentment that had been absent for a full seven years, since her beloved mother, Amy, had ended her life—committed suicide—(we use so many euphemisms to protect ourselves from the truth, Marie always complained!) was returning. In small glimpses at first, and then a bit more often and for more prolonged periods of time. It was the healing retreat he urged her to go on and which Marie did attend that opened the door of her heart again to begin to get rid of some of the guilt and allowed that space to be filled with peace and love instead. 'Oh happy day! Oh happy day!'

That had been a happy day for Amy too, believe it or not. As when Marie's heart had eased from some of the pain, as if by some sheer miracle, Amy also began to feel her guilt easing and the volume of her self-critical voice softening by quite a few decibels as it began to feel overall calmer and a bit more self-forgiving. It seemed at this point that Marie had been holding the key to the gate of heaven and it would not turn and open the door for Amy unless Marie allowed that to happen. Marie would unlock the door eventually for Amy to go through to the next plane . . . or plain? Wherever and whatever that might be? But, how much longer would Amy have to continue to wait? How long would it take Marie to totally and utterly forgive Amy and herself and allow Amy to move on? Once Marie forgave Amy completely, the psychic bond would be severed and both of them would be set free. It was all down to Marie!

The only question that really remained was, for how long? How long would it take for Marie to be set free and consequently set Amy free? How long, indeed Amy mused! She hoped against hope that it wouldn't be another seven years.

Alas, it would be another seven years, but neither Marie nor Amy knew at this stage. All they knew was that their pain had been easing and the suffering softening as their hearts were slightly lighter, their faces softer, their minds freer, and they both could perceive a light at the end of a long dark tunnel.

Chapter 14

The church bells were ringing their hearts out. They were ringing loud enough to wake the dead! And so they had. She was not allowed any respite and was much more awake than she had been for a long time. She watched as the people gathered in front of the statue of Our Lady of Lourdes. The choir was singing. The church was packed, and this wasn't her funeral, thank God! 'Well, thank God all you want,' Amy mused, 'but He hasn't made an appearance yet, honey and goodness itself only knows when He will!' It was just about seven years, and the number seven had been very significant in the Catholic church, perhaps still is. In the Old Testament, she remembered the seven years of abundance and the seven years of famine, the seven years in Tibet (hang on, that wasn't in the Bible!), the Master had ushered his disciples to forgive not seven times, but seventy times seven, or something like that, the seven days in the week (oh oh, was she getting desperate here?), seven sacraments, seven Acts of mercy, seven years in this state of being she thought would be a milestone, which would make Him appear and judge her.

The bells rang louder and the crowd cheered as the statue left the niche in the church and began to be moved by some very strongly built men out of the church. It would make a rendezvous around the village with some devout people following, while others would be getting drunk staggering home in the early hours. The village festa she had loved. Not the outward trimmings of all the flags being hung up along the narrow and busy town streets, but the 'inside' part where people prayed the Rosary, sang hymns, knelt for hours, and prayed and prayed and prayed. She was one of the exceptions and she did pray from the bottom of her heart. She had not cared what people thought of her, had she? She would sit at the third pew from the front on the right-hand side of the village church all dressed in white and pray and pray and pray for forgiveness, for peace, for a cure, for an easy way out but most of all, she would pray to die! She would pray for that 'grace', for that 'gift' every single day without fail. And every morning she woke up would shake her faith, as her prayers would not have been answered. She had often wondered if He had actually heard her prayers at all. What was wrong with her prayers? Why hadn't they ever been heard and even more pressing answered?

Ironically, the more she had prayed to die, every single day without fail the healthier she seemed to be, physically at least, much healthier than her contemporaries. No asthma, no eczema, no arthritis, no rheumatism, no menopause, no physical aches and pains, no glasses just a few grey hairs, low blood pressure at times and apart from that a completely clear bill of health. Who would believe it? She yearned to go to the doctor's and be told she had a terminal condition which only gave her a few days to live. She longed for a truck to crush her to pieces. She prayed for a bolt of lightning to strike her. She wished an escaped convict would shoot her. She dreamt that the people who were producing illegal fireworks whom she had shown up to the law would pursue her, and after torturing her (that would purge her of her sins and make her justified before she enters the kingdom!) would throw her already badly mutilated body over the cliffs. Why hadn't any of this ever happened to her? Why was she so alive and well, when all she had ever wanted was to die?

Now, being on the other side, she began to realise, isn't that great either. Or hadn't been up until now. Seven years! And in these seven years, she had to look at her life, little by little hoping that perhaps she were halfway there. 'Hopefully,' she thought! Looking at a life she hadn't been proud of. But, also made—or so it seemed to happen spontaneously as there had been nothing else to do—to look at the impact the way she had chosen to live her life had had on those around her.

Up until now.

She was suddenly touched to see her Marie there at the village festa. She didn't think Marie had ever been into the village festa. But, alas, there she was with her two good-looking boys. Marie was transfixed looking at the statue's face as if in deep prayer (and she probably had been), but the boys were making signs (not rude signs at least!) to one of the statue bearers. Of course, how dumb could she be. It was none other than her hazel-eyed beloved son. He hadn't been into the village festa either if her memory had served her right. And her memory at this point in time had been the best it had ever been, to her detriment, of course, as the things she had been so keen to forget kept coming back as clear as daylight.

He had been offered this prestigious position of front statue bearer by his then boss who had strong connections with the church. Not necessarily with the Maker himself, but he knew people, who knew people in the right places who could procure one, not anyone, of course, such an honour. And there he was in honour and remembrance of his beloved mother who had been dead for seven and a half years, as he knew how devout she had been to The Lady of Lourdes.

And by his side, supporting him as usual, walking alongside him every step of the way was Marie with her two boys. Marie hadn't stopped loving her brother like a son, and although he was a grown man of twenty-five, she still couldn't help feeling partially responsible for his happiness and well-being. She had felt guilty that she had got married just six months after her mother's passing away and leaving him and her beloved dad to fend for themselves. Not that they had not been capable, of course. Mike made it seem like he wouldn't cope but he did just fine and took care of her hazel-eyed son as much as she would have done. And although this son was now twenty-five, Mike would still cook for him, clean after him, and iron for him. They were a right pair, those two! A right pair! Never saw eye to eye, every conversation ended up in an argument, but they loved each other and Mike did like a father would always love a son.

The son, however much he loved his father, held a bitterness up to this day, a bitterness that ate into his heart and stopped him from returning his father's love. It's true Mike had always painted a picture of how he had been the perfect dad when the kids were younger. But both Marie and her brother knew and had seen a very dark side to Mike, a dark side he had hidden well from the rest of the world.

So, the son held on to the terrifying images of when Mike came home drunk, swearing and tearing the furniture apart. Not just the furniture, though. He was tearing the family apart. What neither Marie nor her brother knew at that time was that he was breaking down as his heart had been shattered and his world had crumbled down when he had found his beloved Amy in bed with his best friend Greg, never to be the same. The anger, the hurt, the pain he had to endure day in and day out, neither of them knew. All they knew was that he had terrified them, and when he would have one of his violent outbursts and sometimes lash out at Amy, they would freeze with terror, not knowing if she would be alive or dead when he had finished.

The son had never allowed himself to forget this. He would not forgive, and he would not forget. Alas, the bitterness had still been eating him up inside little by little, insidiously! Marie, on the other hand, having been a person searching for God, searching for meaning, and trying to live a life of love had been able to forgive. Mind you, the memories were there, but the pain and the power of those memories over how she felt was nil. Nil. Gone. Kapput. And she had been able to love her dad and embrace him nonetheless.

He was a good man. Not once had he spoken ill of Amy. Not once did he mention to either Marie or her brother what had happened in the land

Down Under. Not once did he make the children think any less of her. But the lashings out were not just from the pain of what had happened in the Land of Koalas and Kangaroos—that he had been willing to let go little by little over the years, albeit in very small doses.

What had been causing the outbursts had been a fresh pain a pain so akin the former that it was making him go insane in his head. He could cope with the idea that Amy had made a mistake in the past, and that was that. But the idea that she might be falling in love with his new best friend on the tiny island shaped like a fish in the middle of the Med was too much for his heart to bear. The way she looked at him, the way she flirted with him. Uncle Don. Uncle Don, who had been the husband of her own best friend and the father of little Susie, not so little now. There she was in a very elegant new dress she had bought for the village festa talking to her Marie. How those two had still remained friends after all the family history, Amy did not know. But, she watched on amused as these two women hugged and chatted and were so genuinely pleased to see each other.

Nobody had ever found out whether Amy had actually had an affair the second time around with Uncle Don himself. Flirt she did. Even Marie at only ten years of age noticed how her eyes lit up every time he entered the house, and how pleased she had always been to see him. She couldn't help smiling whenever he was around, and Marie thought that Uncle Don had lit up something deep inside. But, poor Mike was beside himself at the mere possibility, not that she would be having another affair, but that she might not love him anymore. And if she did not physically have an affair, the possibility that she might want to have one, the possibility that this man could make his Amy happier than he could drove him insane.

He tried to escape from this pain hence the alcohol, the drunkenness, the outbursts, the two jobs a day job, driving a truck for a local company, and a night job fishing. But how can you ever escape from yourself? How? He tried and succeeded most of the time but failed miserably at others. He would hurl verbal abuse at both the children when it all got too much to bear. And, yet again Marie's love for him superseded the hurt, the abuse however, the son's love didn't suffice so he clung on to the hurt, the pain, and to the sense of having been abandoned and rejected by one who should have protected him, been there for him, and not having had to be protected by Marie from him.

She wondered whether her son and Marie were at the festa to remember her. Neither of them had seemed to have bothered before. Alas, things change and people change. People change? Do they? Had she ever changed? She was as hard-headed as an Easter Island statue and as unforgiving as the cold weather in Antarctica and wouldn't change. But she was changing now. What use was it changing now, anyhow? Did it count? Was this what all this watching and waiting was meant to procure? Maybe. Just maybe.

When embodied, she had resisted change with all her might. Now, without realising seven years down the line she had changed. Maybe not enough to be fully justified and made pure to see His face, but much more pure and aware than when she had first entered this state of being. She, for one thing, began to realise that although she had known the source of her illness, didn't know that it mostly boiled down to not having been true to her heart. Not having been true to her heart, not once, not twice but many times. She perceived that her unhappiness and her depression had come from having made the wrong choices for the wrong reasons—the wrong reason being that it was the choice that went against what her heart had been telling her. How sad. She had done what her father would have liked her to do to settle down, have a family. She would have loved to have become a school teacher and had the acumen and the brains. Alas, she married to please and get rid of her dad, but not a man she had loved. Being true to her heart would have taken courage, faith, and strength, which she could now see in Marie, but they were qualities she had sadly not taken the time to develop and nurture. The path she had chosen had then taken her further and further away from where her heart wanted and needed to be. And it took her seven years in the afterlife to realise this. The realisation didn't come without any pain, of course. And like many good things in life, it required a death of some sort, for a new life to begin to blossom as the pain began to subside with each new realisation and whenever she admitted to a truth. It also came in stages and not necessarily in the right order, either, if there was a right order as sometimes it all seemed to be happening at once. Then, there would be a gap, a space and then more things happening. It was hard to analyse and rationalise it all. So it was best not to, but to just allow it all the happen, to unfold.

The truth will set you free. She'd been down this road. These words had already been ringing incessantly in her ear. Hadn't a philosopher also said that one needed to 'Know Thyself'. Maybe you had to know yourself so that you could have the audacity to love yourself followed by the courage to be true to yourself. But this wasn't easy, and it took a lot of courage to look, strength not to falter and lose heart at what you find, (as there might be things deep down in the recesses of one's heart one might not really warm to!), and faith that it is all part of a bigger plan with a purpose and it will all be all right, only if one trusted in one's heart, the seat of all wisdom, the oracle that answered all our questions if one dared to look inside, to be still and to look and listen.

Wow! How come her Marie had been doing all of this already in some shape or form? She had to give her Marie much more credit than she had thought. Her Marie had much more courage, strength, and faith than Amy had ever had herself. She had underestimated her eldest daughter's capacity for authenticity by a long shot. However, Marie wasn't there yet and still sadly had a long way to go but she on the right path which was a step in the right direction and Amy was emboldened by that thought on her daughter's behalf.

And Marie continued to follow the statue, with her two tanned, lively sons and her lifelong friend Susie, her eyes shining with love and faith. It pained her to perceive that Marie had outshone her in this respect but still had a few home truths she would have to face up to one day. Not now, not today but soon, much sooner than she thought. Marie would have to continue to look as she had been doing. Marie would have to continue to search as she had been doing. But Marie would also have to look closely at what she found. And when she found it and didn't like what she found, as she maybe hadn't been true to her heart like her mother before her, what would she do? Would she have the courage to face it and act? Or would she run and hide? Or despair?

Amy joined Marie in her prayers. And as Marie looked into the Virgin's eyes and prayed for the soul of her departed mother and beloved brother, Amy prayed that Marie would be true to her heart and have the courage to live according to her original purpose. She would require a lot of courage to do that as after years of looking and not liking what she sees, she will be faced with a choice, to act or not to act, to move closer to where her heart was taking her or to continue to shun her heart's voice and move further and further away. Those will be questions only Marie would be able to answer and decisions only Marie would be at liberty to make. In the meantime, Amy would have to watch, powerless to change anything or anybody so as to make Marie's life more bearable and help her be true to her heart. That was a pain only a mother who loves her children and a father who dotes on his children can know—to have to sit back and watch utterly powerless—powerless to do anything in the face of a situation in which the child might require guidance, courage, strength, and faith. Amen.

Chapter 15

Marie had always had the gift of hiding. It was amazing how she hadn't been hide-and-seek champion in her childhood. It had been Marie's favourite game, especially since Uncle Don's two sons who Marie had adored (well adored one, and was adored by the other!) also played, as did half the street. Marie loved hiding and had always found really good spots to hide her tiny body. It seemed that she continued to enjoy this game even in adulthood, especially when it came to hiding pain.

She had continued 'business as usual' over all these years and over much more than seven years had passed. Amy had nearly lost count until it was Marie's birthday and realised that what had seemed like an eternity had only been nine human years of waiting in total. But Marie had now had the boys in primary schools, secured a primary school teacher's job in one of the boy's schools, retrained, and was getting on with life. She always seemed so happy, so upbeat as if she hadn't ever had to carry any weight on her shoulders. As if she were still just nine or ten years old, young, lively, carefree, and full of energy. And so she was. She was blessed with an abundance of energy for sure. Yet, inside she still carried a pain. Hidden deep inside, the pain lingered and loitered and wasn't going to go anywhere in hurry. The guilt, for something she hadn't done—she hadn't killed her mum; she hadn't failed her mum; she hadn't been the key reason for her mum's suicide—had began to subside especially since through Fr Nicholas and some counselling, her head and her heart became reconciled to the fact that there had been nothing she, or anyone else, for that matter could have done, that she hadn't done to prevent her mother from taking her own life. She, Marie, had in fact been the reason why Amy had hung on for much longer than she had intended to and nothing that Marie had done or hadn't done would have made any difference on that day.

As Marie began to accept this, changes began to happen in Marie's heart and mind. On the one hand, it was liberating—to realise that it had been her mum's decision, and only her mum could have made that decision for various reasons of which were not all known to Marie—and Marie had began to accept that. It was a slow process, but Marie began to absolve herself of a crime she did not commit. She began to forgive herself for not having been psychic and not knowing that Amy would make that decision on that day. She began to forgive herself, believing that she had done all that she could have humanly done for her beloved Amy. She began to see that there had been a bigger picture and that Amy's reality must have been unbearable to make her commit such an atrocity. It began to dawn on her that in a funny, weird sort of way (manipulative, contriving, and controlling!), yet, her mother did love her and had tried to put her first before herself even many years ago.

She began to feel less angry towards Amy and grew in compassion as she herself, now being a mother of two, was able to put herself in her mother's shoes. Motherhood and fatherhood, for that matter, weren't a trifle easy at the best of times, let alone when the adults are struggling with guilt, pain, loss, rejection, and are totally where they do not want to be and shouldn't be. Far removed from their original purpose in life, the treasure to where their hearts would lead them.

Marie began to understand little by little the plight of parenthood, the giving up involved, and what it takes to love unconditionally, accepting and embracing other human beings whilst expecting nothing in return. Expecting nothing in return when in a good place is bearable, but expecting nothing in return when you feel, as Amy did, that you had given your life and soul for that child is another. Expectation is an awful thing, a bind but sometimes we cannot let it go and it becomes harder to love and accept the people in our lives just as they are and expect nothing in return, and Amy could attest to this.

Marie continued to feel lighter inside and the peace she had known in her youth continued to come in longer bouts. She continued to be blessed with courage to search for the truth, the strength to look, and faith in the process and in life and in her God whom she believed loved her with an unconditional love, would not let her perish, and would support and sustain her in her pain and anguish and darkest of hours. And so it had been. And as Marie continued to heal inside so did Amy. Amy too was able to judge herself less harshly and now that her daughter, the person she had loved the most and subsequently hurt the most when here on Earth, was healing so was she. How amazing! It still felt as if Marie held the key to the heaven Amy still hoped she would go to one day. It would be Marie that would set her free!

And yet they continued to journey together. Unbeknown to Marie, of course, that Amy was closer to her now than ever before—knowing the pain in her heart, healing when she is healed, yet in pain and suffering when Marie was suffering. And suffering there was in plenty.

Alas, it seemed as if her Marie who had wanted to be liberated from the past, from the pain, from the suffering and continued to take refuge in her faith, prayer, and then more recently in Yoga and in meditation couldn't see the light at the end of this tunnel. This was another long, dark tunnel in which Marie and The Man had been walking very slowly towards . . . nowhere. Since they had travelled abroad, they had travelled separately, each going their own way. It is very lonely being in a marriage where one of the spouses goes one way and the other goes the other way. Amy knew this as did so many women who kept this pain of a loveless, lonely marriage very close to their hearts, divulging it not even to themselves. Others, hack it and it doesn't seem to bother them. Marie wasn't sure it bothered The Man, either. As far as he was concerned, he came home to a gorgeous wife, lovely children, a clean and tidy house, and a freshly home-cooked meal. The rest was neither here nor there. That his heart had grown cold over the years and distant from that of Marie's didn't seem to bother him at all.

It did bother Marie though. It ate at her. She felt the cold gulf between them widen and deepen and was scared, always very scared. She also felt powerless in the face of this cold, callous heart as the closer she had tried to get, the further away The Man's heart would go. When she made an effort to take a step back, perhaps put in a little less effort, create some space, the heart would soften slightly yet, it was too unpredictable, too unstable and she never knew where she stood and it ate her inside. Little by little, the boundless reserves of love began to be drained and patience (a great virtue, not just in a marriage!) began to wear thin, as the sense of togetherness was lost. 'Would it ever be found again?' Marie questioned every waking hour of every wakened day. 'Indeed, would it ever be recovered?' Amy wondered too.

Although unlike her father before her she had never caught The Man in bed with another woman, she knew in her woman's heart that she hadn't been the love of his life. He lusted after many a woman and flirted with many a girl and deep down Marie had known that the love (in some shape and form) that had once bound them together, allegedly forever, was dead. As dead as a dodo. As dead as her mother had been. Or not quite, as Amy was still hovering about watching as this sad saga unfolded hoping that her daughter would be true to her heart if The Man wasn't and couldn't be.

It made the space where Amy's heart used to be ache with an unbearable pain as she had to watch, but completely unable to interfere, to do anything to make things right. Would things have been different had she still been there? Would she had been able to help her daughter then? But The Man had been so hell-bent on marrying her Marie (whether he had loved her or not that would be another matter for another day), that it would have been hard to have had stopped the marriage. She had actually hoped that her death would be more effective in stopping the ceremony from going ahead and that if that hadn't worked, then possibly nothing would have done.

The ache in Marie's heart grew stronger, and she could not deny it. With every heartbeat, there would be a throb of pain, at the reality that had hit her. It was a struggle sometimes to be true to your heart, to know what to do for the best and what would be right as there were also many other voices in her head wanting to be heard, clamouring for attention, and they too claimed that they were real, valid, and true. How would she be able to tell them apart? How would she know if she were listening to her heart and being true to it, when the voice of The Man echoed that it was all her fault in her head, the voice of the church shouted in her ears that the bond of marriage is forever and that there are *no* exceptions to the rule as mental and emotional bullying (verging on abuse didn't count, the voice of family questioning her judgment, her own voice asking whether it would be justified or not to listen to her heart what if her heart had got it wrong? It was a massive risk which she wasn't sure she would ever be able to take. It required a courage she wasn't sure she possessed, a faith she was scared she would fall short of.

Yet, she continued to teach in various schools, various classes, various children of various ages. She continued cooking various food, on various occasions for The Man, the boys, and anyone who cared to pop over for a Sunday lunch. She continued to take the boys to various after-school activities, at various places, on various days, and at various times. She continued to make new friends and go to various places, attending various courses and doing various voluntary activities. And, so it seemed life went on, and from the outside, it seemed like a rosy existence. This beautiful woman, with a handsome husband, two healthy boys, in a small but cosy house (which Marie always maintained she had turned into a home), on the outside was a picture of perfection. To an outsider's eye, this was the perfect model of a modern loving family in which everybody would live happily ever after. But, not to Amy! Amy knew better. Amy watched as the tears streamed down Marie's face every time The Man came home late, giving her not just the cold shoulder, but a cold, unrelenting heart. Amy watched silently, as Marie's heart gave out so much love that over the years there had not been any left to give. The Man would take that love but not give anything in return. He was very measured shall we say in how much he gave. At times, it felt to Marie as if he was giving her the crumbs left over from his sumptuous banquet, and they would not satiate Marie's need for love, acceptance, and recognition. He did not share Marie's zest for life and passion for whatever she undertook.

In the end, Amy had to watch powerless and didn't have a clue how to replenish and heal her daughter's heart as all the love had been wiped clean of it and there had been nothing left, but an empty vessel making no sound but the sound of sadness, pain, loss, and death.

All Amy could do was to watch and pray and pray and watch that her daughter would not be destroyed by the cold and callous and cavernous space in The Man's being called a heart. This was indeed a torment for Amy and yet, Amy—knew now more than ever before that this is what is meant by purgatory and this is the way her soul would be purged and made pure and clean ready for when after being totally purged, she would be welcomed into his kingdom—could watch, but do nothing about what she saw.

Marie would never be able to comprehend the extent to which The Man had actually damaged and hurt her, which was just as well as it would make it easier for her to forgive him one day when the day and time were right. She prayed that just as Marie had forgiven her, had forgiven Mike, and was becoming more and more healed more and more free and more and more liberated she would eventually when all was said and done be able to forgive The Man for his transgressions which only he knew the extent of (and Amy, of course) so that one day Marie would be totally and utterly free.

Amy longed to see that day. And the amazing thing was that she wasn't keen to see that day so that she, Amy, would also be liberated (or so she was beginning to conclude), but because she couldn't bear to see her daughter continue to suffer so much. It was becoming very clear that her daughter who had been capable of so much love hadn't got much love in return. She had been able to embrace Mike, The Man, and her Amy unconditionally (most of the time, anyway not always), yet nobody had been able to do that for her. Not up until then, anyway.

No, actually there had been people. Marie's grandma—Grandma Jo—Amy's mum. Amy recalled the pure love that had existed between her own mother and Marie. Marie had always felt totally and utterly loved by Amy's mum, and her grandma knew how much Marie had loved her and loved her totally in return. She would look out for her and, most of all, soothe her when upset, troubled, and hurt. Amy's mum had been a source of strength and support for Marie and made up for what Amy failed at miserably. Amy's mum and Marie were like a bright light of goodness and love shining in each other's world.

Amy's eldest brother had been another. For the first four and a half years when Marie had inhabited the land Down Under, he had lavished unconditional love like nobody thought was possible on Marie. She had been the centre of his universe and his love the kind that gave and gave but never expected anything in return set Marie up for what she would endure later on in life. Not, that he did not get anything back from Marie. Marie, from her very nature, had always been very generous with her love and affection and returned tenfold the love her uncle had lavished on her throughout their time together.

The leader from the centre had been another. He had loved Marie and believed in her too, God rest his soul. It had been as if God had sent these two people into Marie's life to affirm her goodness, her capacity for love, for teaching and for being a ray of sunshine in a cold and bitter world.

Amy did not know, and neither did Marie if The Man ever did love her Marie. The Man had not had much love in his life either. Discipline and control had abounded in his upbringing, but warm yet strong unconditional love, acceptance and trust had not loomed large in his family home. Amy didn't know whether to feel sorry for him or whether to judge and condemn him at times. He definitely did not possess the strength, courage, and faith that her Marie did and in that respect she pitied him. However, his arrogance, social snobbery and pride made her want to judge him. But judge him she could not, as being on the other side, it would delay her purgatory for an indefinite period so she had to choose and she would choose to pity him, as that made it easier to forgive him.

As for Marie, she knew in her heart that she did not come first in the Man's heart (infact, she came after money and financial security, his career and after the other women he lusted after), and hiding this pain deep down in her heart, she continued business as usual trying to lose herself in the hustle and bustle of her busy daily schedule trying to numb herself against the pain at times. At other times mustering the courage to look, watch, and stay with that pain trying to uncover the source trying to come closer to the truth, hiding at times behind masks, hiding behind excuses and blame and then coming closer again and then retreating in fear until one day she could not hide from the truth any longer and it seemed like her heart would be shattered.

Amy watched astonished as her daughter came the closest she had ever come to the truth, to acknowledging that the Man had not loved her and that she had had no love to give to The Man any longer, to any man for that matter as her reserves had been depleted and she had run out. She had been running on a nearly empty tank for many years but had not acknowledged it as it hurt, yet this time, she did not try to hide from the emptiness inside and she faced the pain full on.

'Will she act on this?' Amy mused. If so, when and what will she do? Amy had a few more years in waiting now but not many more as Marie came closer to the truth, it would set both of them free.

Chapter 16

Marie woke up that morning prepared to repeat the ritual she annually held at the anniversary of her mother's death. She had come a long way in terms of her inner life and had let go of as much pain and suffering as one could humanely let go in so many years. It would be fourteen this year. Fourteen years in purgatory for Amy and fourteen years of having gone to hell and back for Marie. Yet, both women were the most healed they had ever been now fourteen years down the line.

It had been a sunny day. Yet, neither of the women would have guessed that this would also be a memorable day. Not because Marie had lost weight, not because Marie's grey hairs had turned back to black (as she had incessantly prayed, but in vain naturally), not because suddenly Marie were a rich woman (which she was having her health and two lovely sons), not because the sun had been out either, but because today unbeknown to either of the women a miracle would happen! Miracles are scorned at in our day and age.

It's funny how many people don't believe in miracles, and yet we are faced with the miracle of birth every second of every day, with the miracle of a sunset and sunrise every day, with the miracle of health, with the miracle of oh, many people would just call it life but, maybe life is a miracle that needed to be celebrated every day. Not just on special occasions, like a birthday, an anniversary, Christmas, Easter, summer holidays, Diwali, Eid,

Yom Kippur. Amy did promise herself that if she were ever allowed to come back, she would celebrate each and every day as if it were her only one. She had wasted so much time moping about the past, moaning about the present, fretting about the future that next time she would, she vowed to herself, live in the present moment and be true to her heart. She would also make sure that she did not hide from the truth as the truth will set you free the words came back.

What else would she do differently? She would make sure that she showed the people she loved, how much she loved them each and every day. She would embrace and joyfully accept any love bestowed upon her, which she had never allowed before and would equally allow her love flow forth to all sentient beings.

She would sing loudly in the shower and dance naked in the house! She would eat, drink, and be merry. But, she wouldn't smoke. She would make friends and not keep herself to herself, as a recluse. Good friends made you happy and she would be a good friend the next time around, given the chance. She wouldn't sleep with her best friend's husbands as that caused too much grief, for them and for her.

She would, on the other hand, allow herself to make mistakes as unfortunately that's how we all learn. She would allow herself this blessing of learning from her mistakes and not beat herself too much about it. She would smile, accept her 'mistake', sin, transgression call it what you will. Ask for pardon *not* just from a higher being as she had done but from herself and do her best not to do it again and to do what is in her power to make it right.

She would try basically and simply to do good and avoid doing evil. To love herself, as she realised she couldn't love anybody else unless she had loved, accepted, and celebrated herself. She would love herself, embrace herself in her totally. She would celebrate who she was and do her best to see herself as she really is. To see reality as it really is, not how she would like it to be. To live in the present, let go of the past, and not live in the future.

After loving herself, accepting herself, and forgiving herself, she would be able to love, accept, and forgive others. It took her a whole fourteen years on the other side to realise all of this, whilst her Marie through a lot of soul-searching was there already. Not there literally as being enlightened, but aware at least that this is what she should be doing and doing it to the best of her ability.

How would she love herself? She always had associated loving herself with being selfish as did so many of her contemporaries. She would set boundaries and not let others take too much or much more than she could give. Give when and how much she can but not more. Not selfish, just protecting myself! She hummed to herself.

She would do more of the things she had enjoyed doing, rather than just the things she was told she ought to do so she'd spend more time dancing, singing, eating out, socialising rather than church cleaning, going to church twice a day, praying the rosary four times a day, and reading the Bible forever. She would do these things as they helped her faith, but in moderation. Everything in moderation. 'I would need to live,' she thought. 'I won't hide behind the ritual, the law, the rules to protect me from living from feeling the pain, from taking responsibility for my actions, for an excuse to hold on to the pain hiding behind the guise of "being good" as I obey the law!'

The law does not justify you, she realised. The law protects you but it does not justify you. It is love that justifies one in the eyes of God. That she realised now. Love. That four-lettered word, used and abused over the centuries, is what lies in the depths of each and every one of us. It is the love we have for ourselves, for others, and for a God, if one is so inclined, that will save us. A love which allows us to search and find, look and see, and take responsibility as fully fletched adults for our actions and their consequences. Love is what The Master had said is what His Father looks at, the love one has given out. When asked about whether the prostitute should be stoned, Amy remembered reading that His words were, 'She has been forgiven a lot as she has loved a lot.' It wasn't because she had obeyed the Law, it was because of the love in her heart that she had been saved. In fact, Amy realised that her heart had been cold, numb, and dead and that obeying the Law did not revive it. Maybe, that's why her prayers for healing were never answered. It's not that they weren't answered, it's that her heart had been so far away from love and so immersed in self-absorption, self-centredness, self-cherishing which she hadn't acknowledged, of course, when down here on Earth that it couldn't be healed. Only people who acknowledged the pain and watched and waited in this life with love burning deep in their hearts would allow healing to take place. They knew what was going on in their hearts and wanted their hearts to be healed and it would. She had seen it happen to Marie many a time.

Yet, when one knew what their heart wanted and needed but chose not to look and watch and wait and see, but numb the pain of a broken and banished heart with pills then, no amount of prayers could procure the healing. The healing came from acknowledging the pain and looking and acknowledging, wanting to be healed. The Master had always asked people what they wanted before He actually laid hands on them to heal them, even though He himself knew that they wanted to be healed. He waited as they acknowledged the desire to be healed and then went ahead and procured that healing whether it was a blind man, a paralytic, an old woman, a mentally ill person—he would always check how badly they had wanted it after having acknowledged it.

Amy didn't really want to be healed, did she? Did you, Amy? No. She felt she had needed to punish herself for the rest of her life for her transgressions and didn't deserve to be healed and to be made whole. She knew what her heart needed and wanted, but wouldn't allow it to have it, as it didn't deserve it. Yes, next time, against all odds she was adamant she would love herself, embrace herself (even the bits she did not particularly like about herself), allow herself to make mistakes, and forgive herself the mistakes she makes as she had believed that Her Father in heaven would.

What was that smell? she wondered. She hoped Marie wouldn't set the house on fire. This daughter of hers, she knew had loved her with all her heart. It was a shame how in spite of all her selfishness Marie would never know how much Amy had actually loved her how much she had owed her and how much she actually owed to her. But what was that smell that mad woman she was always up to something.

Of course, it had slipped Amy's mind that today was the anniversary of her death. Marie had always performed a ritual either on the day itself or a few days prior depending on whether schools had broken up for the holiday or not. Marie wasn't keen to perform her annual ritual with the boys in the house. It was a private affair one which a mother doesn't share not even with her offspring. It was the candles she had been lighting in every single room in the house; there had been a candle burning.

It was a sunny day. The candles were burning in every room. Fourteen long years of watching and waiting for Amy. Fourteen years of searching, praying, and healing for Marie. Both in each other's minds and in each other's hearts! The love that Marie had lavished on Amy which she had thought had been wasted, thrown away in anger and in ingratitude was there burning in both their hearts . . . It had not perished . . . It was what had saved them both!

Chapter 17

The candles burnt slowly yet surely as Amy would have said when embodied. The sun was still out, albeit fainter than she had ever remembered it in any of the places she had lived. The house was spotless the windows cleaned, the furniture sparkling, the dishes done, the clothes ironed and all in all, a picture of domestic bliss. She believed that Marie had been a bit OCD about cleaning, but hey, who was she to point fingers? It was a bit of the pot calling the kettle black, as she herself had been quite obsessed with having a sparkling clean house. It was ironic, though that Marie who had so rebelled against it was now exactly the same. Very house proud extremely house-proud indeed! It was partly a cultural thing, and partly a personal thing as if the cleanliness of the house reflected the cleanliness of the soul the healing, the wholeness inside.

Anyway, what was Marie doing now? She was quite an unpredictable one, she was and had always been, Amy realised now more than ever before after all these years of watching and waiting! Quite unpredictable, feisty, and spontaneous. You were never quite sure what she was going to say next, do next, plan next, what decisions she would make and where she would go. She had exercised the right that every woman is deemed to exercise with no valid reason and at very short notice—that is, of changing her mind. Oh, yes! Amy couldn't keep up with how she decided one thing one minute, was hell-bent on it, but changed her mind the next for no apparent, valid reason. At times such as those, she had actually felt sorry for The Man as he wouldn't have a clue how to take her and what to say and what to do. A bit confusing to say the least for someone whose outer, physical, everyday life had to have structure, a lot of structure.

Marie after having lit all the candles had decided she would pray for the souls of her dearly departed mother, grandmother (although she knew in her heart of hearts, as if as a matter of fact, that her grandma Jo had been in heaven just a few years after her death), and her and her boys. She continued, after all these years, to pray that the psychic link between her and Amy would one day be severed, so she, Marie, would be set free once and for all! Free to be who she was meant to be a woman in her own right, knowing her own heart and maybe one day finding the courage to listen to her heart and do what her heart and gut actually told her she needs to do even though it might be scary, not make complete sense and would throw her into a sea of uncertainty and insecurity. If she were to trust in her heart and be true to her heart, all would be well!

So why hadn't it been all well for her deceased mother? Why? Was it because she hadn't been true to her heart? Is that why in her mother's world, it hadn't been all right? Is that why in her mother's world nothing would and could make it all right? Is that why her mother's story did not have a happy ending, and she did not live happily ever after (in this realm at least!)?

Marie felt fear all through her being, wondering if she would share the same fate. Alas, she sat down in her eldest son's bedroom, on his freshly made bed and prayed. Marie had prayed every day of her life not for wealth and riches, not for flashy cars and big houses, not for prestige, not for fame and fortune but for an inner peace and inner healing for her and for all the people she loved. She prayed that she would be a living beacon of light shining in the dark, spreading love, light, and peace everywhere she went and to whoever she met. But it wouldn't be her peace, her light, it would be the Divine light within her that Divine spark that abides in all our hearts and reverberates throughout the whole of the universe and throughout other universes and other realms and dimensions. She prayed that Divine will use her, as and how is necessary, to bring peace, joy, and love to humankind. She prayed that she will continue to be healed from the wounds inflicted upon her and take responsibility for dealing with the pain these wounds procured. She prayed she would be brave to take responsibility for her own well-being and not be dependent on others to bring about her happiness, healing, and wholeness. She prayed that she would be a good mother lavishing the love she had never had onto her two adorable, beautiful sons whom she had loved more than life itself. She prayed that whatever The Man and she did would not interfere with the plan that life and the Divine had had in store for her two sons and that they too would have peace and joy in their hearts. She prayed for The Man that he would begin to see how far apart they had grown that his perception of what is, is different to what actually had been and that he too would be able to face the truth that is that the love that had once brought them together had died. Some people would say it had changed, morphed into a brotherly and sisterly love. Marie, if she had to be honest with herself, would have to say that it had died. Not, that she would ever wish The Man any harm, definitely not. Not that she hated him, definitely not. But she did not and could not love him in the way a wife should love her husband. She had felt he had betrayed her trust many years before many many times, and as much as she had tried to trust him again and to trust in their love she couldn't. Not that she hadn't tried. By Jove, she tried and tried and couldn't have tried any harder. But, as soon as she would decide to trust again, he would say something and do something to sow the seeds of doubt in her head again. It used to mess with her head so she prayed for clarity to see the truth which would then set her (and him) free. She prayed to forgive him and for him to forgive her and for her to continue to forgive Amy as it felt as if she almost was ready to let it all go!

She burst into tears. This irritated Amy so much, partly because it scared her to see her daughter in so much pain and not able to do anything about it. Partly because it seemed that Marie cried all the time a bit as if it were a habit, a natural reaction to happiness, to pain, to fear, to ecstasy, to anger, and to joy. You could never win with Marie as she would cry when happy and when sad and sometimes you wouldn't be able to tell which one it actually was, so it would leave Amy confused as she looked on.

What was it today? Was she happy, or was she sad? Hang on what was happening to Amy? What could Amy feel tugging at her heart? (Or where her heart used to be!) What was that pulling her backwards and pushing her forwards like in a swinging movement? Amy had loved swings when she was young . . . Oh, how she had loved the swings! She remembered when she would take Marie to the swings, and she, Amy, would also go on it and the two of them would laugh their heads off, as they felt they were being such rebels. She had always felt so young, so free on a swing, especially if there were a breeze gently blowing against her tanned, soft, moisturised skin. It began to feel a bit like that now as if she were swinging and a breeze were blowing and something was happening as Marie sobbed, then cried and then cried even louder praying to be set free.

Her ardent prayers must have split through the heavens and beyond as her lifelong yearning for healing, for letting go, for forgiving and being forgiven were being answered there as she, Marie, felt a presence. She professed she had not seen any flashing lights, like some of her friends boast they see when praying or meditating nor had she been elevated from the mattress neither had she smelt sweet smelling aromas. No, she just felt a gentle presence, movements and a release.

Marie knew beyond a shadow of a doubt that at that moment, she was being set free. Her prayers had been answered and the psychic link was being severed there and then in that bedroom. The sobbing subsided and was replaced by a peace. A gentle, subtle peace began to fill Marie's whole being from head to toe, and from toe to head. She sat there, uttering praises to her God who had been faithful, who had heard her prayers and who had set her free.

It was at this point, unbeknown to Marie, of course, that the key had been turning, and the swinging and the breeze gently carried Amy to the next realm of her existence. She had been absolved by her daughter and hence, able to absolve herself. She had waited and watched long enough, realised all the damage she had caused, acknowledged it, took responsibility for it, began to heal from it, and now was ready to move on to the next stage. Here, she would not be bound by Marie's progress or lack of it to move on or to have peace or to be whole. Here, she would be independent. Here, she would . . . what would she need to do here? What was she there for?

Anyway, suffice it to say that on that sunny day, the sun shone indeed in the hearts of two beautiful women, who had been bound by suffering and pain on opposite sides of existence . . . one embodied . . . one disembodied waiting to be set free . . . and free she was today. Free to roam the Earth, still disembodied with a peace and joy that accompanied having been purged from her sins . . . forgiven by her beloved Marie and forgiving herself . . . being made whole . . . her whole being in a tizzy with excitement! Excited, yet scared at the prospect of the unknown. Unknown indeed! Where was He her maker whom she had waited for a long fourteen years to come and judge her? He had taken His time, but he would come now.

Her guardian angel once again took pity on her lost soul and warmed her with His love and peace and joy and reassured her that she was now in the right place, but not the right time, yet to see Him face to face—not yet, he reiterated!

Chapter 18

She remembered that yellow and blue book of *Catechism Stories,* it had been called. Marie had bought it to help her with her teaching at the local village catechism centre. Amy used to read it daily on the loo and had done for years. Perhaps, there had been a time when she had set herself the task to learn the whole book by heart. She had needed to get a life have some fun and some giggles and laughs some wining and dining, maybe. What had possessed her to try and learn the whole book by rote she couldn't fathom now such a thankless task. But, it had now come in handy . . . aha . . . it hadn't all been in vain . . . Oh, no! It would give her an overview of what would happen or could possibly happen at this stage like a rough guide to the universe, or beyond.

The problem had been that it had got it wrong the first time. It hadn't mentioned anything about waiting and watching all the damage you had caused, to whom you had caused it, feeling their pain, hearing their anguished cries until it seems like your whole being would break. That you would have to acknowledge that that had been your doing, and you would have to accept it.

There was nothing in there saying that if you forfeited taking responsibility for your actions on the other side, the able bodied side, then you would have to do it when disembodied and that it would potentially take much, much longer as you were powerless to act. You had time and all you could was watch and wait and when the weight of the damage you had caused would hit you like a ton of bricks, the book didn't explain how that would feel. It didn't describe how after taking responsibility for your misdemeanours . . . transgressions . . . sins . . . you would have to forgive yourself! That depended on whether the people you hurt had actually also began to forgive you. If they didn't, then you would have to wait for much longer!

There was nothing in the book about the power the people you had hurt had over when you crossed over to the next realm how long you stayed there for and what you would do there! Nothing in the book that was pertinent to her present situation now, or so she thought.

Until it struck her that there was. The next stage was described in the book, but not as a process that would take place in the afterlife it was advocated on Earth. It had been the teachings of her church and she was sure it had been in the book as well, that after one acknowledged the damage they had caused others, wittingly or unwittingly, intentionally or unintentionally they would have to acknowledge it, ask pardon, and be forgiven (and forgive themselves! This wasn't in the book, but she knew for a fact that unless she had forgiven herself at the same time that Marie had done, the women would still be bound in endless pain and suffering!). There was the last and final step that would lead to what? Where? She did not have a clue . . . 'A step at a time,' she thought to herself . . . 'A baby step at a time, Amy! Be patient and all will be revealed.'

Amy thought hard as her guardian angel held her in his arms in a gentle, loving embrace while she figured it out. She felt loved unconditionally for the first time in eons it seemed. She felt safe, secure, at peace, and happy with a warm glow in the place where her heart used to be or is now, as it has been restored.

But, what was that last stage? She couldn't put her finger on it. It was on the tip of her tongue! How frustrating! What would happen if she couldn't remember? Would she be stuck here forever? She still had yearned to see His face and hoped that fourteen years of waiting was enough. But, apparently not. Hey, who was she to make these decisions? What had she been expecting, having given her free will on Earth that He would take it back just because she had happened to cross to the other side? No, He wouldn't; of course, He wouldn't. Isn't that why it had been up to her to absolve her herself, purify herself, and it would be up to her how long it would take to make it up to the people she had hurt to absolve her and be absolved?

So what was it again? She wished when she spoke to Marie, Marie could hear. All she would need to do is ask her the question. Marie always had had the answer when it came to these things and to many more. Marie had known for many years that the fountain of unhappiness and pain in Amy's life had been her not being able to let go, her inability to move on and to forgive herself and be true to herself. It seemed as if Marie could see it as clear as daylight and knew what and how Amy could get better, be healed, and become whole you see. Marie had all the answers but Amy wouldn't listen! She wouldn't see it then! Anyway, she had cracked it now and that was all that mattered.

It had to be one thing, and one thing only! It seemed to be coming to her . . . A . . . it started with an A . . . A . . . for . . . Australia, Apple, Appleford, Ashford, Asbestos, Airborne, Asshole, Aviary, Attest, Attention, Awareness . . . Atonement! Atonement that was it . . . atone for her sins! Atonement not only for the things she did out of selfishness, self-centredness, self-preservation, fear, and a lack of genuine faith but also for the things she could have and should have done, but didn't. Like when she refused to acknowledge her selfish ways, forfeited responsibility of all her actions, and closed her heart to love. How would she know how to put things right? And how long would it take? She wouldn't have a clue where to start!

The only consolation she felt was that at least at this stage, she was at peace with herself and with her Marie and her heart glowed with joy. It was a pinkish, red glow that would light a whole house if needs be. She couldn't remember when she had last felt so content so fulfilled and so peaceful. This was bliss, complete and utter bliss compared to any memory of the past whether before or after her demise.

Here to her sheer and utter surprise, she began to recognise some people. Alas, there were some familiar faces. She wasn't on her own anymore. She couldn't fathom how she had endured her own company, being completely alone for the last fourteen years. And yes, before anybody asked, being on her own, she was lonely too! Not like the caption saying, 'On my own, but not lonely!' It had been a very lonely and painful state where she had been.

It was only now that she realised how much she had missed human interaction, companionship, and possibly friendship—well, how would it work now? As these spirits communicated with each other, with no bodies, no mouths, no tongues, no lips? She didn't know as this was all brand new to her. But she recognised quite a few people there whom she had thought would never make it to this place. She had judged them, and as only God knows what resides in the recesses on one's heart, she had judged them wrongly—or misjudged them as we say.

Some other familiar faces she was pleased to see and smiled at the prospect that this could be a very happy place indeed and hoped that she wouldn't have to leave this place in a hurry. She wouldn't be on her own whilst atoning for her selfishness, self-centredness, pride, arrogance at thinking that she had all the answers and for closing her heart to love and compassion for herself first and foremost and for others. For refusing to live in the present moment, accept things as they were in the present moment, accepting herself and people as they were in the present moment, acknowledging the damage she had caused, forgiving herself and letting go but above all, as she had said to herself time and time again—for not being true to her heart! It had been called 'mental illness', but she wasn't sure herself how much of it was actually mental and how much spiritual (if you could completely separate and isolate the two, of course!).

Alas, she wouldn't be on her own while atoning for the damage she had caused as she endeavoured to make it right! Maybe there would be others who would help her and she would help them in return, of course, having learnt from Marie whilst she had watched her all those years that it was all about 'give and take'. 'Give and take,' Marie would reiterate to her two handsome boys, trying to drum it in like a crucial skill to have in life. A good skill, perhaps virtue if you like?! Although, to Amy's mind, it wasn't the ultimate virtue as that would be to give and not to expect anything in return! But, for the time being 'give and take' will do.

It all then seemed so strange that as Marie had acknowledged in her heart of hearts that she had been set free, she seemed to know also that at exactly that same time, her mother had been set free too. She had felt it in her bones—the fact, that her mother was now able to move on to where she needed to be, to a better place where she wouldn't have to suffer so much anymore. She had done enough suffering and endured enough pain for many lifetimes and now was the time where she would go to pastures green, to a land of milk and honey where manna would fall from the sky to satiate her hunger and fresh running water gushing out of rocks would quench her thirst.

What Marie did not know is that Amy would be very close to her. Very close indeed! What Marie was unaware of was that Amy would find a way of letting Marie know how much she had actually loved her, how sorry she had been for hurting her so much, and that Amy would be around doing her best to make things right. This Marie was unaware of and had no way of knowing, apart from the fact that in heart of hearts she always felt so protected by a higher power, not only by her God, but also by a host of angels and good souls who seemed to surround her with love, lots of love and boundless energy.

Little did Marie know that on that day, The Man too had also been touched by all of this . . . grace?! That day he said, when he came home from work, he had felt strange during the day. very strange inside. Strange, how? Marie had asked and at about what time. He had said it had been some time before noon. He too had been touched, how Marie did not know, but he had felt a nudge, and for the first time in many years apologised for the hurt he had caused Marie and asked for forgiveness. Asked to be forgiven owning to the fact that he had hurt Marie terribly through thoughts, words, and actions. It was a happy day! Another happy day, indeed! Marie couldn't believe her ears. These words she had been yearning to hear for years; they were being uttered on that very same day. That day The Man had got a glimpse of remorse as something had touched his heart which had been opened. And Marie did not want to shut it back up, to demolish this spark that seemed to ignite after years of darkness said she would forgive him, of course she would.

Over the years, she tried to forgive him his transgressions as they went along, but it had been hard sometimes as she felt so desolate, abandoned, and unloved. She would forgive him, but he would have to atone. He would have to try to make things right! It's not that she had been perfect ! As much as she aimed at perfection, she had had her downfalls too. Hadn't she always been so bitter about emigrating poisoning their bond with insidious resentment? She had apologised many times over the years for her transgressions and had really tried to make the most of it, to not be too bothered about being cold all the time, missing the warmth of the sun but mostly missing the warmth of a loving, tender, and caring heart.

They tried to agree on the best way forward but couldn't see eye to eye on how The Man could put things right. Whilst Marie was keen to go on a couple's weekend retreat with him to rediscover the spirituality that had bound them so delicately and sublimely together, he was keen on going to counselling and so to counselling they did go.

And although Amy would watch now, she would be able to see but not feel the pain of Marie. Whatever she saw would not hurt or harm her in any way anymore. She had earned her restful state at long last and the peace she had now been blessed with was there to stay. It wasn't going anywhere. It was a constant that accompanied her wherever she chose to roam with whoever (and this got very exciting, suffice it to say!), whenever!

She would watch, and very quietly, subtly, unobtrusively intervene *only when needed*. She would know she was told by her guardian angel, she would know when intervention was needed and allowed—she would know. She would have to be true to her heart and follow her heart and gut faithfully so that all would be well.

She was told (by her guardian angel, once again) that she wasn't allowed to influence any decisions Marie would make or change the course of Marie's destiny, or destinies but, she would be allowed to protect Marie, and her boys. She would be allowed to be nearby, showering them with love and light and filling Marie with courage and strength. She wouldn't be allowed to stop Marie from making mistakes, but when Marie did make mistakes, she would help her get back on her feet in some way or another and help her get up quicker, heal sooner than she otherwise would have. Marie had to learn her lessons in life too, Amy acknowledged that. As painful it would be for Marie, it wouldn't hurt Amy anymore.

At least now, nothing that happened on Earth had the power to affect or diminish her sense of peace and well-being. It was not that she cared any less or loved any less. It was that now possessing such inner freedom from expectation, self-centredness, self-absorption, she could love more unconditionally not expecting anything in return as she made things right.

It would take a while, but Amy was now not in a rush to go anywhere. The warm glow in her heart love, true love sustained her and would take her to where she needed to be. She would trust that with all her heart. On the other hand, she also knew that she would see His face one day, but unlike her mother who had seen His face and was with Him singing to the children in heaven not long after she died, she still had unfinished business to attend to. And she would, for as long as it takes. Sustained by this constant peace, joy and sense of calm, tranquillity and well-being which nothing or nobody could take away she would joyfully restore her Marie as her Marie had restored her on this day.

Chapter 19

Don't get me wrong, this state of being wasn't a doddle, but compared to any other form of existence, it was heaven. It wasn't a walk in the park either. Although a walk in the park was possible at this stage and lovely parks too. She thought the Savill garden was a nice one to wander about, especially when Marie, The Man, and the boys were visiting. The lush vegetation, the variety and the fact that it was so well tended, even lovingly tended she might add. The colours, the smells, the actual vision of beauty and the lushness of life, attested to the Earth's thirst for life that was not easily satisfied.

Actually, it wasn't a heaven on Earth, not a heaven in Heaven but, a heaven somewhere, somewhat, somehow. She would get there one day—to heaven that is, for the moment, this would suffice. The one good thing about this state or realm as it were, was that she had been allowed to sleep. Sleep and rest from the days of work. Well, that wasn't the only thing, was it really? There was also the fact that time didn't stand still here as you watched, and waited for what seemed like forever! Time actually went very fast and sometimes she couldn't keep up with so many friends to meet for lunch, damsels in distress to save, dances to attend to, posh dinners to grace her presence with, accidents to prevent, world leaders to try and illuminate, social justice to procure, drug addicts to protect, prostitutes to embrace in love, victims of war, disease, viruses, and gas poisoning to strengthen . . . and the list went on and on. Healing, the whole world was in need of healing. She would do her bit for humankind with a heart glowing with love and overflowing with generosity and compassion she would. But, most of all, she would be spending time making it right to her Marie—that was her priority. The other priority was her newly found love, more of that later.

First things, first however. Up until now, Marie hadn't had it easy in any respect as Amy saw now with eyes wide open. Her past had been trying enough as it was, her present painful and sad and her future? Only God knew her future, but occasionally Amy got a glimpse and hoped and prayed that Marie would one day be all right. That one day, like her, Marie would be happy, light in body and spirit, free from anger, afflictions, fear, and anxiety. Loved and able to love in return, appreciated, respected, accepted. Loved unconditionally. How she would play her part in all of this hadn't as yet been made clear to her but she would aid Marie in any way possible to bring her to a safe and happy place of healing, restoration, and peace. A bit like allowing her a foretaste of heaven on Earth!

The warm glow that glowed in Amy's heart now, that love glowed in Marie's heart too! So, although sad and in pain, confused and not knowing where to turn to, where to go and how to get there, Marie was inwardly strengthened by this warm glow which she believed to have been the Love of the Divine living within her. She attributed her success in her studies, in her role as a mother, in her career, in her friendships to the strength that that glow gave her. It failed when it came to her marriage but alas, Marie soldiered on sometimes with a stiff upper lip but, most times with a twinkle in her eye and a love and strength in her heart. Her heart knew that Marie was getting closer and closer to changing her life forever and coming closer and closer to what her heart's deepest desire had been and so the heart was strengthened, the burden lightened, and the way became clearer.

Amy watched like a mischievous monkey wanting to play with Marie, letting Marie know she was there, interfering in situations where it mattered, poking her nose in, minding Marie's business but, she hadn't been allowed. She would only be allowed to reveal herself to Marie once Marie had made the final decision—to stay, or not to stay in her soulless unhappy marriage, that is the question Marie had to find the truthful answer to.

Amy had wanted to shout, whisper, sing the answer into Marie's ear or do whatever got Marie to listen. Oh that girl could be so stubborn sometimes! And Amy had been finding it very hard to keep her opinions to herself and not to butt in. So she eventually enrolled the help of friends to tell Marie that in actual fact she should leave The Man and start a new life on her own with her two lovely boys. Much less damage in the long run, when looking at the bigger picture, would be done to all concerned if she found the courage to leave—damage litigation Amy would call it. She wanted to reassure Marie that her suspicions weren't unfounded and that she hadn't been going mad but would if she stayed much longer.

Unfortunately, none of her newfound friends were allowed to relay this message to Marie either! Marie had to stand firm on her own two feet and face this demon on her own. So, Amy would sometimes choose a song, a number, a word, a friend who said that which would be her thoughts exactly. How apt and close to cheating it had been, but all is fair she seemed to remember in love and war.

She would hope Marie would read into messages left on billboards and notice boards, and sometimes when she got desperate, it would be the clouds, the sky even. Marie wouldn't know that that gentle breeze on the day she had been heartbroken would have been Amy gently caressing her face, trying to reassure her that she would pull through this in one piece. She had hoped that the lovely smell of the roses in her tiny front garden would tell her how much she was being loved by a benevolent and generous universe and by her dearly departed ancestors. Hadn't Amy always maintained that she would make a much better mother when she had crossed over and now was her chance to make it right. She hadn't in the first fourteen years been able to keep that promise unfortunately, due to unforeseen outcomes, but now within what she were allowed to do, and with what she could get away with, she would fulfil that promise with every breath she would take. That can't be right, can it? She stopped in her musings to listen to her breath, but no sound came, and there was no movement either. She only realised now that she had breathed her last many, many years previously a fraction of a second just before her unsuspected body had been smashed and turned into a pulp!

Anyway, she observed how Marie's inner strength that came from various sources, but mainly from her faith in a loving, forgiving, and all-embracing Divinity, continued to grow. As her own daughter went from strength to strength, Amy became more and more hopeful that Marie would find within her what it takes to be true to her heart. Amy believed that in spite of the fear of the unknown, the opposition The Man would put up to Marie and him physically going their separate ways (notwithstanding the fact that they had been going their separate ways in other ways for the last ten years or more anyway!), Marie would pull through if she took the plunge acting on the what she knew in her heart of hearts she had to do. But would she actually take the plunge? Would she, like her mother, by rather metaphorically than physically jump off the precipice into the dark unknown? Amy, like everybody else, wondered but could only watch, and her guess would be as good as anyone else's.

As for herself and her own happiness, Amy was overjoyed. It seemed as if, if you did not make it on Earth in finding your soul mate and were stuck in the next realm up (there were many more realms but Amy would have to wait. Some saintly people like own mother were just taken straight to heaven!), she would be united with them in that state eventually. Amy had never read about this in any book, and the Catechism Stories book certainly did not cover this possible aspect of the afterlife. And neither did her church. If still on Earth and exposing such ideas, she would have been deemed a heretic (and mad) and possibly ex-communicated! She had been quite ostracised in her lifetime for endorsing some radical views at the time. She would have been deemed a witch and burnt at the stake in the middle ages surely, but sadly people on the tiny island she lived on still had pretty tiny mindsets.

Anyway, Marie had always known how much Amy had liked Uncle Don. Uncle Don had lived on many years after Amy had gone. But, one thing, no two things actually had remained with Uncle Don after her suicide. The first was a rubber plant which Amy had especially propagated for him from her own one in the little internal yard she had owned. He had loved that rubber plant and especially after her death, hung on to it for dear life as if he could still feel her alive through the tree near him. His wife had urged him to get rid of it as she knew like every other woman knows when her husband is in love with someone else. Eventually, he had to relent and the wife got her way. The tree went and instead their internal yard hosted a myriad of luscious, colourful plants that pleased the eye and rested the senses, but bore no link to the deceased Amy.

So then he had to stick to the second thing that had remained and that had been the love in his heart. Encouraged by the vivid memories of all the special moments they had shared, not just physically, but intellectually and spiritually, his love for her lived on in the depths of his being. The words she had uttered when they would be together would resonate in his head with the same accent, the same sweet intonation, and the same softness. He thought his heart would break when he had heard the news of what she had done. And the news on that day had spread like wild fire throughout the four corners of the island, or rather from the island's mouth to its tail, throughout the gills and spread through the fins.

To say he had been shocked is an understatement. He thought that the bond that had existed between them would save her. A bit like her Marie, he had hoped his love would be enough, but it wasn't. He too had felt betrayed and rejected. And although throughout the years their encounters were less in number, they were by no means any less intense and passionate. It was just that they had been watched like hawks. She, by her husband who although had grown to trust her over the years, at times still did turn up at home unexpectedly, between jobs for a cuppa and a bite.

Him, by his extremely suspicious wife who had been Amy's best friend once. Amy thought about this as if his wife had no right to be suspicious. His wife had every right to be suspicious, and she was actually right in her assessment of the situation. Just because she hadn't caught them in bed, in the act, didn't diminish how he had felt for Amy and his wife knew it. Arguments ensued. Words were said. Tempers flared. Yet, as they did in those days, they stuck it out, until he died. It was many years after Amy's death—too long to his liking as he longed to join her wherever she had got to. His wasn't self-induced; no, it was a debilitating illness which struck and with a vengeance only an illness can show killed him.

Amy had continued to look on as he had been ill and didn't like seeing him like that. But she had been unable to help. It had only served the purpose of highlighting how awful it can be watching someone you love suffer so much pain, change beyond recognition, wither, and then eventually die. Her Marie must have felt like that many times when having cared for her, it had made her wonder, and although she hadn't withered physically, mentally there had been not much left at the time.

Uncle Don had been a good man. Not as strong as Mike. Mike was good and strong inside and was able to endure pain and love through the tears and the rejection. Uncle Don, as she preferred to call him (it was his pet name on Earth), was a good man, but his life had been quite straightforward. He was kind. He was generous. He was spiritual. He was intellectual. Very good looking, but not as good looking as Mike, either. But, somehow, somewhere down the line, she fell for him, and he fell for her and that was that. Life did get very complicated after that, as how do you hide it from the other people who love you and whom you profess to love? But, more importantly, what happens when you hide it from yourself?

Uncle Don, unlike Amy, hadn't hidden it from himself. He acknowledged it. One could go as far as to say, he embraced it. He did not beat himself about it. What he did do was try his best not to act upon it. He tried to continue in his actions to be loyal and faithful to the wife he had promised years earlier he would. He was saddened that his heart didn't feel the same way towards his wife, but there had been nothing he could have done about it. He stopped having sex with his wife—as he had thought that wouldn't be being true to his heart. His sexual appetite wanted only to be satiated from one source, and if that was impossible, then that was that—otherwise, it would be as if he were using his wife to serve his own needs rather than from desire to show her his love. He had also stopped sleeping in the same bed as his wife. He wasn't completely honest when he had blamed it on the extent of her consumption of booze, but anyway, he thought it was more honest to sleep on his own rather than fill his wife with a false hope that one day he would make love to her, or begin to even love her again. Sad really. Really sad.

It was the closest he had come to being honest. It was all well and good having tried to get Marie to be true to her heart and to herself, but in her and Uncle Don's days and in their culture, you didn't really. Well, you did, to a certain extent, to the extent that it was socially acceptable; otherwise you would be deemed as a disgrace for your family and by society. So, in a way it was a compromise he had reached. Him and his wife knew that there would be no sex, and that meant that the love had died, if not in the heart of both parties at least in the heart of one of the two. You slept in different beds, you did different things. Uncle Don had kept up the appearance until his children were much older and continued to do the family days out. But, when the children all three of them flew the nest, that stopped. And he wouldn't go out with his wife. Not to church. Not to the café. Not to the Tombola (he hated the Tombola). Not to her mother's. Not to her sister's. Nowhere.

Chapter 20

It had been the village festa, and as like the endless cycle of life and death it came every year without fail, and with it Marie came back to the island with her two growing sons to visit for the summer. Not just to visit and sight see, of course, but to pay her respects to family and friends. Sometimes, it had been pleasure, at others a chore.

This year Uncle Don sat outside his front door from where he could see the statue being ushered around the town, surrounded by his wife and some of his children. Unbeknown to him, and to everyone else, no doubt, this would be the last summer he would do this. As the following September, his illness would get the better of him, and he would die. He didn't mind. Instead of trying to fight death, he embraced every single living day he was given, strengthened by the fact that he had lived—oh, yes! He had lived. He had travelled. He had loved. He had taken risks, worked hard, read avidly and had fun—he had lived. And to one who had lived and has no regrets, death is not so daunting but just a passing on to the next stage.

He was consoled by the fact that he had always tried to do the right thing too, out of a love and generosity to others. He was one who would always try to put the shoe on the other foot and make sure that nobody suffered unnecessarily and alone. He had always loved his children from the bottom of his heart and would have done anything to stop them from being in pain and suffering. He respected his wife. She had been feisty, loud, loved drinking, and dancing, not very intellectual or spiritual (like Amy had been), but he had loved her once and respected her always. They were different, very different but together they had brought up three beautiful children and that was not something to be scorned upon.

Marie, as friendly and as lively as always, went up to him for a chat. She had always been intrigued by this man of few words, who always seemed so calm, serene and at peace inside. She had always respected him and silently wished him and her mum would have been able to make a go of things, as they would have been so compatible. In this case, partner swapping would have been ideal but, alas not something their culture would have condoned, or their church for that matter!

Little did either of them know that this would be the last chat Marie would ever have with Uncle Don. Little did she know that Uncle Don would still play a part in her life—well, not hers directly, but indirectly in some shape and form. Little did either of them know what lay ahead. Both, both of them, were uplifted by their little friendly hug as they watched the statue approach down the road. Amy's hazel-eyed son still bore the statue on his broad, tanned shoulder as he had done now since Amy had died. Marie would go and follow the statue and walk alongside her beloved brother in a minute just as she had done every year for many years. But, first things first. To finish this little encounter with Uncle Don before they would both move on. Chit chat, chit chat and friendly goodbyes and off she went. And off he would be soon, too!

They chatted a little bit about his illness and how he wondered how long he would still be here for. He explained to Marie that he didn't really fear death, although what the next stage beheld, he did not have a clue. *The Plain Truth* (a magazine him and Amy had been into for a few years) had had many plain truths in it, but the magazine like Amy's 'Catechism Stories' did not give you much that you could go on, on what happens to your spirit when your body gives in, either through old age or through illness or through an intentional or unintentional accident. It did speak about heaven, but more like a heaven on Earth a bit like a Garden of Eden, a Paradise here on Earth which wasn't going to happen anytime soon. So he wasn't sure, as none of us are, really what would happen to spirits departed until then!

He decided to keep an open mind, and that whatever would happen he would be supported by the fact that he had tried to live a good life, doing good, as is humanely possible avoiding doing evil and hurting others. He had tried to be as true to his heart as much as it had been socially and morally acceptable in his time—people of his children's generation have so much more freedom to achieve that. And he had loved (he never wished his wife any harm) his wife and his children with all his heart.

What he did believe and felt quite sure of was that he was Divine (had a soul) and the Divinity within him would live on and move on to where it needed to be, until finally it would be united to the Universal Divinity. Not that the two were ever separate, they had always been one! But having a body had created the illusion that they were separate, and he believed that one day there will be no obstacle (be it the physical body or sin, as it were) that would divide the two up. That was his idea of heaven.

The village festa had come to an end, and so had his life just a few weeks later. He was calm on his deathbed, serene and looked almost angelic. Not knowing what to expect next, but not too bothered by it. It can be a very uplifting experience watching someone die with no fear of the unknown and no fear of what they are leaving behind. No fear of the uncertainty of where they are heading. No fear. No anger about having to leave and what and who they were leaving behind. Resignation. Not quiet desperation, but a calm, serene resignation—acceptance of how things are!

So imagine his surprise when, not having had to spend too much time watching and waiting, (nowhere as near as Amy had done) he saw Amy! His beloved Amy had made it to this place, or this state after all! Not many people would have thought she would have, as suicide was frowned upon in her church and it was debateable whether it believed that they would make it to that place or not. Anyway, there she was looking all coy and shy, smiling. He didn't remember her with long hair; she had always worn it short on the island. And, she looked so much younger too. He had always thought she looked beautiful, not plain, but beautiful, very beautiful. But now he couldn't keep his gaze off her, and the glow in his heart began to pulsate not just with love, but with excitement and passion.

He didn't know that these sensations would still be possible on the other side. He felt alive inside, much more alive than he had done in years. She'd lost weight too. He wasn't sure he remembered what a good pair of legs she had had. That pink miniskirt and white lacy strappy top really suited her with her red lipstick and red painted toenails. He actually thought he hadn't really known her taste in clothes, colour, and make up at all. Not that any of that mattered. What mattered now was that his gaze was resting on the object of his love, which had been denied him for a long time, too long.

He was being rewarded, but for what he wasn't sure. He didn't expect after this waiting that things would get this good. This was a realm of no suffering. It's true one had to atone for their misguided decisions here on Earth after they had seen them in the watching and waiting place and had to make things right to all the people they had wronged, but it was OK. You didn't get to do it alone, you had company, you had friends and everybody helped everyone else. Moreover, he (lucky thing) had a lover, a friend, a soul mate. And he was happy, a very happy man indeed.

He was a man of a few considered, well-chosen words and would not say two if one would suffice, but on this day, there was nothing that could stop him talking. On this day, it was as if he had wanted to condense a lifetime into a moment and tell her everything. Everything that had gone on while she had been away. But, most of it she had known already. Not that she would say so, of course. She listened intently, as the red glow in what used to be her chest began to pulsate within her, and the love denied by society and social convention and condemnation decided it would not be denied any longer, could not be denied any longer not in this realm—in this realm everybody had to be true to their hearts. In this realm, souls were real . . . authentic . . . true to themselves.

Neither of them knew how many realms there actually were. The rumour ruled it was seven, and seven to her seemed a logical number of realms only because she had thought of the seven years she had spent watching and waiting . . . no, not seven actually seven times two! Then there were all the other sevens which she had known but had escaped her now, as they seemed so irrelevant as she was ensconced in his warm and loving embrace.

What they did know was that the realm of watching and waiting (in which it needs to be added he only spent about the equivalent of a human year in, if that) was the second. The first realm which they both had skipped was the 'lost souls' realm. The 'Lost Souls' would wander and search for peace in the wrong places, knowing they needed to get to the waiting and watching realm, but not quite knowing how to get there. That realm was for people who lacked complete awareness in this lifetime. There was complete and utter selfishness and self-absorption to the detriment and physical and emotional harm of loved ones and everyone else. People who were totally and utterly proud and arrogant, thinking that nobody else had anything that they could possibly learn from. People who would judge and misjudge others using very harsh measures and being very unwilling to look at themselves. People who had shut their eyes, their ears, and their hearts to love, unable to put themselves in someone else's place. People who hung on to hurt, to pain, to suffering, and would not let it go allowing resentment, anger and even hatred to fester and fill their hearts. People who obeyed the Law went to church, prayed, fasted, but gossiped, judged, and were not kind and compassionate, patient, and forgiving. It boiled down to those who had shut their hearts to love; the love of a higher being, the love of others, and to the love of themselves.

Amy could have ticked quite a few of those boxes herself, but she had not closed her heart to love, and although to love had been an effort (so according to Marie it wasn't love as love should flow freely from the heart) she had tried to do the right thing by everyone, she had been kind, she had shown compassion many times, if only she had shown compassion to herself. She had loved and she had loved her children more than herself, and more than she could ever let them know. But she was determined she would let Marie whom she had hurt the most know. Somehow she would and she wouldn't give up trying. Marie had to know how much she meant to her, and how much she hadn't wanted to hurt her. She had glimpses and saw the damage on Earth unlike the 'lost souls' who had never even allowed themselves to glimpse!

Anyway, the 'Lost souls' weren't her problem at the minute! What was her problem? Now, she had Uncle Don on board. He would help her on her mission to relay her message of love and forgiveness and to help her atone and make it right to Marie! Now she wouldn't have to do it on her own. She had help, she had reinforcements, and she had what she had never had on Earth a soul mate. She had her own sweetheart, her friend, her lover and it was all legitimate. Her soul mate and her were united now; they were one. 'They were one in spirit and nobody and nothing would ever split them up as they travel together through all the realms to come,' Amy smiled to herself.

As she would endeavour to make things right with Marie, she would have Uncle Don by her side a blessing she hadn't counted on. As she was in that realm, she would be loved, honoured, and respected as she had always longed she would. Her soul's thirst for acceptance, communication, and communion with a loved one would be satiated. Not how it would be in the final realm, the realm of Heaven, where her soul would merge once and for all with the soul of the Universe, the universal soul, her God, ultimate and infinite Light and ultimate and infinite Pure Love, Acceptance, and Forgiveness. She would have to wait many human years for that, but it didn't matter she could easily accept things as they are in this state. All will materialise when the time is right. This was bearable, much more than bearable in fact, it was a state of ecstasy.

Neither Amy nor uncle Don knew when they would be made to choose whether to go back to Earth or move onto the next realm. Neither of them were partial to the former option, and Amy had vowed to herself, over and over again, that if ever faced with that choice, she won't ever go back. She had paid for her sins on Earth in the waiting place, atoned for them in this realm and it would be her turn and time to move on and perhaps, one day see Him—her Lord, her God, face to face. She still longed for that state when He and her would be one. But, at the moment, she was so blissfully happy being one with her soul mate that it didn't really matter that much, what came after this and how long she would be here for.

In the meantime, they would lay on the beach naked, listening to the gentle lapping of the waves as they sung them a lullaby. He would gently comb his fingers through her dark, long hair as his lips brushed against her hot, flushed cheeks. Their lips would meet, as would their moist tongues and full lips, and as their eyes meet, the red glow at their heart centre would grow fiercer, stronger, and hotter. His hands would caress her silky, smooth nakedness and it felt right. What was she talking about? Right? Of course, it wasn't right, it was goddamned perfect!

Epilogue

She had never thought she would be the one who would have the fairy tale, happy ending which would say '. . . and they lived happily ever after!' No. She had believed she would be undeserving, forever. Yet, she had paid for her sins, seen what she had done, taken full responsibility for it, opened her heart to love and compassion, and was on the way to making things right for her beloved daughter. Her atonement, when complete, would take her through to the next realm. She would be kept busy over the next many years trying to make things right, but there would be no rush as the journey was as valid as the destination, she always had believed.

As for her Marie, it wasn't pleasant to watch. At times, she felt a pang of . . . she wasn't sure of what actually but, it seemed like Amy now having come to undisturbed happiness and bliss had left Marie behind in a sea of misery. She would, by hook or by crook, make it right to her, and now, it won't be just her, but Uncle Don would be there by her side to help too. She would make it up to Marie so that both women who had suffered so much, perhaps sinned so much yet loved so much would be set free from the binds of generations of sin and both would be able to enjoy the peace, the love, and the joy which He had promised would be a gift given to 'men of goodwill' and, as Amy had always thought, to women too! 'Liberation would come,' Amy mused, 'not just to me, but to my beloved Marie!'